William—An Englishman

by

Cicely Hamilton

Double 9
BOOKS

1919

William—An Englishman
by Cicely Hamilton

ISBN: 978-93-69073-01-6

Published by

DOUBLE 9 BOOKS

2/13-B, Ansari Road
Daryaganj, New Delhi – 110002
info@double9books.com
www.double9books.com
Tel. 011-40042856

ABOUT THE AUTHOR

Cicely Mary Hamilton was an English actress, writer, journalist, and suffragist who played a vital role in advocating for women's rights in the United Kingdom. Born on June 15, 1872, in Paddington, London, she was the daughter of Denzil Grant and Mary Ann Hamilton. Her literary and theatrical works reflected her commitment to social reform, with a strong focus on gender equality. Hamilton is best known for her feminist play How the Vote Was Won, a satirical yet powerful work that follows a male anti-suffragist whose opposition falters when the women in his life collectively strike, revealing the impact of women's labor. Another significant play, Diana of Dobson's, critiques economic disparities and champions women's independence. Beyond writing, Hamilton was an active campaigner for women's suffrage, contributing essays, speeches, and theatrical performances to the cause. Her influence extended to her work as a journalist and her advocacy during wartime, where she continued to champion equality. She remained a key figure in feminist movements throughout her life, leaving a legacy of activism and art. Hamilton passed away on December 6, 1952, in Chelsea, London, at the age of 80, remembered as a pioneer for women's rights and an enduring literary voice.

CONTENTS

CHAPTER I

William Tully was a little over three-and-twenty when he emerged from the chrysalis stage of his clerkdom and became a Social Reformer. His life and doings until the age of twenty-three, had given small promise of the distinction of his future career; from a mild-mannered, pale-faced and under-sized boy he had developed into a mild-mannered, pale-faced little adult standing five foot five in his boots. Educated at a small private school in the suburbs of London, his record for conduct was practically spotless and he once took a prize for Divinity; further, to the surprise and relief of his preceptors, he managed to scrape through the Senior Cambridge Local Examination before he was transferred to a desk in the office of a London insurance company. His preceptor-in-chief, in a neatly-written certificate, assured his future employers that they would find him painstaking and obedient—and William, for the first six years of his engagement, lived up to the character given him. His mother, a sharp-eyed, masterful woman, had brought him up to be painstaking and obedient; it might be said with truth that as long as she lived he did not know how to be otherwise. It is true he disliked his office superiors vaguely, for the restrictions they placed upon his wishes—just as, for the same reason, he vaguely disliked his mother; but his wishes being indeterminate and his ambition non-existent, his vague dislike never stiffened into active resentment.

It would seem that the supreme effort of passing his Cambridge Local had left him mentally exhausted for a season; at any rate, from the conclusion of his school-days till he made the acquaintance of Faraday, his reading was practically confined to romantic and humorous literature. He was a regular patron of the fiction department of the municipal lending library and did not disdain to spend modestly on periodicals of the type of *Snappy Bits*. He was unable to spend more than modestly because his earnings, with the exception of a small sum for fares and pocket-money, were annexed by his mother each Saturday as a matter of normal routine. The manner of her annexation made discussion singularly difficult; and if William ever felt stirrings of rebellion over the weekly cash delivery he was careful never to betray them.

With his colleagues of the office Tully was a negligible quantity. He was not unpopular—it was merely that he did not matter. His mother's control of the family funds was no doubt in part accountable for his comrades' neglect of his society; but his own habits and manners were still more largely to blame, since besides being painstaking and obedient he was unobtrusive and diffident. There was once a project on foot in the office to take him out and make him drunk—but nothing came of it because no one was sufficiently interested in William to give up an evening to the job.

The crisis in his hitherto well-ordered life came when his mother died suddenly. This was in October 1910. William had gone to the office as usual that morning, leaving his mother apparently in her usual health; he returned in the evening to blinds already drawn down. A neighbour (female) was in waiting in the sitting-room and broke the great news with a sense of its importance and her own; she took William's hand, told him with sniffs that it was the will of the Lord, and entered into clinical details. William sat down rather suddenly when he realized that there would be no one in future to annex his weekly earnings; then, shocked by his lack of filial feeling, he endeavoured to produce an emotion more suited to the solemn occasion. Disconcerted by a want of success which he feared was apparent to his audience, he fidgeted, dry-eyed and awkward—and finally, all things considered, acted well and wisely by demanding to be left alone. To his relief the demand was accepted as reasonable and proper in the first moments of his grief; the sympathizer withdrew, wiping her eyes— unnecessarily—and hoping that God would support him. He locked the door stealthily and stared at his mother's armchair; he was a little afraid of its emptiness, he was also shocked and excited. He knew instinctively that more was to happen, that life from now on would be something new and different.... The arm-chair was empty; the masterful little woman who had borne him, slapped him, managed him and cowed him—the masterful little woman was dead! There was no one now to whom he was accountable; no one of whom he was afraid.... He walked on tiptoe round the tiny room, feeling strangely and pleasantly alive.

The next day increased the sense of his new-found importance; his mother had died rich, as he and she understood riches. She had trusted her son in nothing, not even with the knowledge of her income, and after the stinting and scraping to which she had accustomed him he was amazed to find himself master of a hundred and fifty pounds a year, the interest on capital gradually and carefully invested. In his amazement— at first incredulous—he trod on air, while his mind wandered hazily over the glorious possibilities of opulent years to come; the only alloy in his otherwise supreme content being the necessity for preserving (at least until the funeral was over) a decent appearance of dejection. He felt, too, the need of a friend in whom to confide, some one of his own age and standing before whom it would not be needful to keep up the appearance of dejection and who would not be shocked at the babblings of his stirred and exultant soul; and it was this natural longing for a confidant which, on the day following his mother's funeral, led to the beginning of his friendship with his fellow-clerk, Faraday.

The head of his department, meeting him in the passage, had said a few perfunctory and conventional words of condolence—whereto William had muttered a sheepish "Thank you, sir," and escaped as soon as might be. The familiar office after his four days' estrangement from it affected him curiously and unpleasantly; he felt his newly-acquired sense of importance slipping gradually away from him, felt himself becoming once again the underling and creature of routine—the William Tully, obedient and painstaking, who had earned from his childhood the favourable contempt of his superiors. It was borne in on him as the hours went by that it was not enough to accept good fortune—good fortune had to be made use of; and he began to make plans in an irregular, tentative fashion, biting the end of his pen and neglecting his work. Should he chuck the office? and if he chucked it, what then? ... Here imagination failed him; his life had been so ordered, so bound down and directed by others, that even his desires were tamed to the wishes of others and left to himself he could not tell what he desired. The need for sympathy and guidance became imperative; driving him, when the other occupants of the room had departed for lunch, to unbosom himself to Faraday.

In his longing to talk he would have addressed himself almost to any one; but on the whole, and in spite of an entire ignorance of his habits and character, he was glad it was Faraday who was left behind to hear him—a newcomer, recently transferred from another branch and, as William realized (if only half-consciously) like himself regarded by their fellow-clerks as a bit of an outsider. A sallow-faced young man, dark-haired and with large hazel eyes, he was neatly garbed as became an insurance clerk; but there was a suggestion of discomfort about his conventional neatness, just as there was a suggestion of effort about his personal cleanliness. He worked hard and steadily; taking no part in the interludes of blithesome chat wherewith his companions enlivened their hours of toil and appearing to be satisfied rather than annoyed by the knowledge of his own isolation. He had spoken to William but two or three times and always in the way of business—nor was his profile bent over a ledger particularly suggestive of sympathy; William's emotions, however, had reached exploding-point, and the door had hardly closed behind the last of their fellows when he blurted out, "I say," and Faraday raised his head.

"I say," William blurted again, "did you know—my mother's dead?"

"Ah—yes," said Faraday uncomfortably; he believed he was being appealed to for sympathy, and fidgeted, clearing his throat; "I—I had heard it mentioned. I needn't say I'm very sorry—extremely.... I suppose you were very much attached to her?"

William reflected for a moment and then answered honestly, "No."

"Indeed!" Faraday returned, surprised as well as uncomfortable. Not knowing what further to say, his eyes went back to the ledger and the conversation languished. It was William who resumed it—wondering at the difficulty of expressing his bubbling emotions.

"I don't mean to say," he explained with a twinge of remorse, "that I had anything to complain of. My mother always did her duty by me. But we weren't what you might call sympathetic."

"Indeed!" Faraday repeated—still at sea as to the motive of the conversation.

"It was unfortunate," William went on, "but it couldn't be helped. I am sure she was a very good woman." (He said this with the more confidence because, from his childhood up, he had always associated goodness with lack of amiability.) "But that wasn't what I wanted to say. What I wanted to say was, she has left me a good deal of money."

"Indeed?" said Faraday for the third time; adding something about "congratulation." He hoped the episode was over—but William was only beginning.

"I've been wondering," he said, "what I should do—now that I'm independent. I don't want to go on like this. It's a waste—when you've got money. But I don't know how to set about things.... If some one would put me in the way!"

Faraday, raising his eyes from the ledger, met the wistful appeal in William's and imagined himself enlightened.

"I see," he said interrogatively; "then you haven't got your living to earn—you are not tied here any longer? You can direct your own life and take up any line you choose?"

"Yes," William assented, pleased with the phrase; "I can direct my own life—certainly."

"Which," Faraday suggested, "was difficult for you before?"

"Very," said William emphatically.

"And," the other went on, "now that you are your own man you wish to take the line that attracts you and be of some use?"

"Oh, certainly," William assented again—perhaps a shade less emphatically. So far his ideas had run more upon pleasure than usefulness.

Faraday reflected with his chin resting on his hand.

"Why have you asked me?" he demanded suddenly—with the accent strongly on the "me."

"I know so few people," William explained humbly. "I mean, of course, people who could give me any ideas.... I thought you wouldn't mind—at least I hoped you wouldn't.... I know it's unusual—but if you could help me in any way? ... With suggestions, you know."

Again Faraday reflected with his chin resting on his hand.

"I could put you," he said at last, "in touch with people who might help you. I should be very pleased to do so.... Of course, I should like to know more of you first—what your views are——"

"Of course," William agreed vaguely, puzzled partly by the words and partly by the enigmatic manner.

"If you've nothing else to do," Faraday continued, "perhaps you'll come round to my rooms to-night for a talk? Say at half-past eight. We could discuss things more comfortably there."

William, still puzzled by the hint of mystery in his manner, murmured that he also should be very pleased, and Faraday gave him the address—returning forthwith to his ledger in sign that he considered the incident closed for the present. He had a distinctly authoritative way with him, and William, who would gladly have continued the subject, had perforce to be content with wondering what the night's discussion and exchange of "views" would bring forth; an evening spent away from home was so rare an event in his life that the prospect of his visit to Faraday's rooms afforded him food for an afternoon's busy speculation. His own domicile being in the region of Camberwell, he did not return to it after office hours but whiled away the time by dinner at an Oxford Street Lyons—secretly glorying in the length of his bill and contrasting his power of spending what he liked with the old days of doled-out allowance. He rang down a sovereign at the pay-desk, gathered up his change and strolled out of the building with an air—and at half-past eight precisely found himself outside Faraday's lodgings in a mournful side-street in Bloomsbury. A shabby maid-servant ushered him upstairs to a shabby, paper-strewn room where Faraday, pipe in mouth, rose to greet him.

They were not long in finding out that the invitation had been given and accepted under a misapprehension on both sides. Faraday, as soon as he had settled his guest in a chair, came straight to the point with "Now tell me—how long have you been interested in social questions?"

"In social questions?" William repeated blankly. "I'm afraid I don't— — What sort of questions do you mean?"

It was Faraday's turn to be taken aback, and, though he did not say it, his eyes looked. "Then what the devil— —?" William's fell before them nervously, and he shifted in his chair like a child detected in a blunder.

"I'm afraid I don't— —" he said again—and halted.

"Then you didn't know," his companion queried, "that I am 'Vindex' of *The Torch*?"

"I'm afraid not," muttered William, who had heard neither of one nor the other.

"Vindex" of *The Torch* sighed inwardly. He was young, ambitious, fiercely in earnest and ever on the look-out for his Chance; and, the wish being father to the thought, he had momentarily mistaken William for an embodiment of his Chance and dreamed dreams since the morning—dreams of a comrade like-minded and willing to be led, whose newly-inherited riches might be used to endow a periodical that should preach a purer and more violent rebellion even than *The Torch* itself. With the aid of William's three pounds a week—magnified many times over in the eyes of his eager mind—he had seen himself casting the hated insurance behind him and devoting himself heart and pen to the regeneration of the State and Race by means of the Class War. And lo!—as a couple more searching questions revealed to him—in place of a patron and comrade was a nervous little nincompoop, bewildered at finding himself for the first time out of leading-strings, to whom a hundred and fifty a year was wealth untold and who had never so much as heard of the Class War! For a moment he was more than half inclined to be angry with the nervous little nincompoop whose blundering, egoistic attempt at confidence had induced him to believe that the secret of his identity had been penetrated by an ardent sympathizer. (It was an open secret in "advanced" circles, though carefully guarded in the office.) Then, more justly, he softened, recognizing that the blunder was his own, the mistake of his own making—and, pitying William's dropped jaw and open confusion, poured him out a whisky and endeavoured to set him at his ease.

That evening in the company of Faraday and his first whisky was the turning-point in the career of William Tully. Any man stronger than himself could at that juncture in his life have turned him to right or left; a push in the wrong direction would have made of him an idler and a wastrel, and fate was in a kindly mood when she placed him mentally and morally in charge of "Vindex" of *The Torch*. She might, as her reckless way is, have handed over his little soul to some flamboyant rogue or expert in small vices; instead, she laid it in the keeping of a man who was clean-living, charged with unselfish enthusiasm and never consciously dishonest. The product of a Board School Scholarship and a fiercely energetic process of self-education (prompted in part by the desire to excel those he despised) Faraday, when William made his acquaintance, was beginning to realize some of his cherished ambitions, beginning, in certain Labour and Socialist circles, to be treated as a man of mark. His pen was fluent as well as sarcastic, and if his numerous contributions to the "rebel" press had been paid for at ordinary rates he would have been a prosperous journalist.

It was somewhat of a shock to William to discover on the top of the whisky that his new acquaintance was a Socialist; but after the first and momentary shock he swallowed the fact as he had swallowed the alcohol—not because he liked it, but because it was something the narrow circle of his mother's friends would have heartily and loudly disapproved of. This reactionary and undutiful attitude of mind was not deliberate or conscious; on the contrary, he would certainly have been horrified to learn that it was the dominant factor in his existence during the first few weeks of his emancipation from maternal supervision and control—urging him to drink deeply of Faraday's brand of Socialism as it urged him to partake with unnecessary sumptuousness of the best that Lyons could provide.

He acquired the taste for Faraday's political views more thoroughly and easily than the taste for Faraday's whisky. The man's authoritative and easy manner, the manner which stood him in good stead with his audiences, of assuming (quite honestly) that his statements were proven facts which no sane human being could dispute, would have made it impossible for William to combat his opinions even had his limited reading and thinking supplied him with material for the contest. He was impressed with Faraday's erudition no less than with Faraday's manner; and impressed still more when, later in the evening, a colleague of *The Torch* dropped in for a smoke and a chat. The pair talked Labour and International movements with the careless ease of connoisseurs and bandied the names of politicians contemptuously from mouth to mouth—William sitting by in a silence dazed and awed, drinking in a language that attracted by its wild incomprehensibility and suggestion. His mind was blank and virgin for the sowing of any seed; and under

Faraday's influence his dull, half-torpid resentment against the restrictions, physical and mental, of his hitherto narrow life became merged in a wider sympathy with the general discomfort, in an honest and fiery little passion for Justice, Right and Progress. That, of course, was not the affair of one evening's talk; but even the one evening's talk sowed the seeds. He went away from it uncomfortably conscious that as yet he had lived solely for himself, never troubling his head concerning the evils that men like Faraday were fighting to overcome. The manner of his future living was decided for him when he knocked at the door of Faraday's Bloomsbury lodging.

His simple and awed admiration for his new-found friend and faith had in all probability more than a little to do with Faraday's readiness to allow the acquaintance to continue—even a rebel prophet is not insensible to flattery. William became for a time his satellite and pupil, the admiring sharer of his schemes, of his hatreds and laudable ambitions; he read Faraday's vehement articles and accepted each word and line. His very blankness of mind made him an apt pupil, and within a month of his mother's death he was living, out of office hours, in a whirl of semi-political agitation, attending meetings and cramming his head with pamphlets. In three months more all his hours were out-of-office hours; in his enthusiasm for his new creed and interests his neglect of his professional duties had become so marked that the manager, after one or two warnings, called him into his room for a solemn and last reprimand. As it happened, Faraday, the night before, had confided to William the news of his approaching appointment to the post of organizing secretary of the Independent Socialist Party, an appointment which would entail a speedy retirement from his hated desk in the City. The news, naturally, had not increased the attraction of the office for William, in whom the spirit of revolt had already fermented to some purpose; thus, to the infinite surprise of his superiors, who had known him hitherto as the meekest of meek little clerks, the threat of dismissal failing improvement was countered by a prompt resignation as truculent as William could make it. In fact, in the exhilaration of the moment, he treated the astonished representative of capitalism to something in the nature of a speech—culled principally from the writings of "Vindex."

From that day onwards he devoted himself to what he termed public life—a ferment of protestation and grievance; sometimes genuine, sometimes manufactured or, at least, artificially heightened. He was an extremist, passionately well-intentioned and with all the extremist's, contempt for those who balance, see difficulties and strive to give the other side its due. He began by haunting meetings as a listener and a steward; Faraday's meetings at first, then, as his circle of acquaintance and interest widened, any sort of demonstration that promised a sufficiency of excitement in the form of invective. The gentlest of creatures by nature and in private life, he grew to delight in denunciation, and under its ceaseless influence the world divided itself into two well-marked camps; the good and enlightened who agreed with him, and the fools and miscreants who did not.... In short, he became a politician.

As I have said, at the outset of his career he modestly confined his energies to stewarding—to the sale of what propagandist bodies insist on describing as "literature," the taking of tickets, ushering to seats and the like; but in a short time ambition fired him and the fighting spirit thereby engendered led him to opposition meetings where, on Faraday's advice, he tried heckling the enemy speakers. His first and flustered attempts were not over-successful, but, sustained by revolutionary enthusiasm, he refused to be crushed by failure and accompanying jeers and held doggedly on to his purpose. Repeated efforts brought their measure of success, and he began to be marked by his comrades as a willing and valuable member.

Within a year, he had found his feet and was a busy and full-blown speaker—of the species that can be relied on to turn on, at any moment, a glib, excited stream of partisan fact and sentiment. His services were in constant demand, since he spoke for anything and everything—provided only the promoters of the meeting were sufficiently violent in their efforts to upset the prevailing order. He had developed and was pleased with himself; Faraday, though still a great man in his eyes, was more of an equal than an idol. He was wonderfully happy in his new, unrestful existence; it was not only that he knew he was doing great good and that applause uplifted him and went to his head like wine; as a member of an organization and swayed by its collective passion, he attained to, and was conscious of, an emotional (and, as he thought, intellectual) activity of which as an individual he would have been entirely incapable. As a deceased statesman was intoxicated with the exuberance of his own verbosity, so William was intoxicated with the exuberance of his own emotions. There were moments when he looked back on his old life and could hardly believe he was the same William Tully who once, without thought of the Social Revolution, went daily from Camberwell to the City and back from the City to Camberwell.... As time went on, he was entrusted with "campaigns" and the stirring up of revolt; and it was a proud day for him when a Conservative evening paper, in connection with his share in a mining agitation, referred to him as a dangerous man. He wondered, with pity for her blindness, what his mother would have thought if any one had told her in her lifetime that her son would turn out dangerous.

As a matter of course he was a supporter of votes for women; an adherent (equally as a matter of course) of the movement in its noisiest and most intolerant form. He signed petitions denouncing forcible feeding and attended meetings advocating civil war, where the civil warriors complained with bitterness that the other side had hit them back; and his contempt for the less virulent form of suffragist was as great as his contempt for the Home Secretary and the orthodox members of the Labour Party. It was at one of these meetings, in December 1913, that he met Griselda Watkins.

Griselda Watkins, then a little under twenty-five, was his exact counterpart in petticoats; a piece of blank-minded, suburban young-womanhood caught into the militant suffrage movement and enjoying herself therein. She was inclined to plumpness, had a fresh complexion, a mouth slightly ajar and suggestive of adenoids, and the satisfied expression which comes from a spirit at rest. Like William, she had found peace of mind and perennial interest in the hearty denunciation of those who did not agree with her.

On the night when William first saw her she wore, as a steward, a white dress, a sash with the colours of her association and a badge denoting that she had suffered for the Cause in Holloway. Her manner was eminently self-conscious and assured, but at the same time almost ostentatiously gracious and womanly; it was the policy of her particular branch of the suffrage movement to repress manifestations of the masculine type in its members and encourage fluffiness of garb and appeal of manner. Griselda, who had a natural weakness for cheap finery, was a warm adherent of the policy, went out window-smashing in a picture-hat and cultivated ladylike charm.

She introduced herself to William after the meeting with a compliment on his speech, which had been fiery enough even for her; they both considered the compliment graceful and for a few minutes exchanged sympathetic platitudes on martyrdom, civil war and the scoundrelly behaviour of the Government. Even in those first few minutes they were conscious of attraction for each other and pleased to discover, in the course of their talk, that they should meet again next week on another militant platform.

They met and re-met—at first only on platforms, afterwards more privately and pleasantly. William, when his own meetings did not claim him, took to following Griselda about to hers, that he might listen entranced to the words of enthusiastic abuse that flowed from her confident lips; he had heard them all before and from speakers as confident, but never before had they seemed so inspired and inspiring, never before had he desired with trembling to kiss the lips that uttered them. Griselda, touched as a woman and flattered as an orator by his persistent presence in her audience, invited him to tea at her aunt's house in Balham; the visit was a success, and from that evening (in early March) the end was a foregone conclusion. Their friendship ripened so fast that one night at the beginning of April (1914) William, escorting her home from a meeting, proposed to her on the top of an otherwise empty 'bus, and was duly and sweetly accepted.

There were none of the customary obstacles in the way of the happy pair—on the contrary, all was plain sailing. William's original income had for some years been augmented by his earnings as a speaker, and Griselda's parents had left her modestly provided for. Her aunt, long since converted to the Movement (to the extent of being unable to talk of anything but forcible feeding), smiled blessings on so suitable a match and proceeded to consider the trousseau; and after a little persuasion on part the wedding was fixed for July.

CHAPTER II

The mating of William and Griselda might be called an ideal mating; theirs were indeed two hearts that beat as one. With each day they were happier in each other's company; their minds as it were flowed together and intermingled joyously—minds so alike and akin that it would have been difficult, without hearing the voice that spoke it, to distinguish an utterance of Griselda from an idea formulated by William. Their prominent blue eyes—they both had prominent blue eyes—looked out upon the world from exactly the same point of view; and as they had been trained by the same influences and were incapable of forming an independent judgment, it would not have been easy to find cause of disagreement between them. There are men and women not a few who find their complement in their contrast; but of such were not William and Griselda. Their standard of conduct was rigid and their views were pronounced; those who did not share their views and act in conformity with their standards were outside the pale of their liking. And this not because they were abnormally or essentially uncharitable, but because they had lived for so long less as individuals than as members of organizations—a form of existence which will end by sucking charity out of the sweetest heart alive.

It was well for them, therefore, that their creed, like their code of manners and morals, was identical or practically identical. It was a simple creed and they held to it loyally and faithfully. They believed in a large, vague and beautifully undefined identity, called by William the People, and by Griselda, Woman; who in the time to come was to accomplish much beautiful and undefined Good; and in whose service they were prepared meanwhile to suffer any amount of obloquy and talk any amount of nonsense. They believed that Society could be straightened and set right by the well-meaning efforts of well-meaning souls like themselves—aided by the Ballot, the Voice of the People, and Woman. They believed, in defiance of the teachings of history, that Democracy is another word for peace and goodwill towards men. They believed (quite rightly) in the purity of their own intentions; and concluded (quite wrongly) that the intentions of all persons who did not agree with them must therefore be evil and impure.... They were, in short, very honest and devout sectarians—cocksure, contemptuous, intolerant, self-sacrificing after the manner of their kind.

They held, as I have said, to their own opinions strongly and would have died rather than renounce, or seem to renounce, them—which did not restrain them from resenting the same attitude of mind and heart in others. What in themselves they admired as loyalty, they denounced in others as interested and malignant stubbornness. More—it did not prevent them from disliking and despising many excellent persons whose opinions, if analysed, would have proved nearly akin to their own. William, for instance, would all but foam at the mouth when compulsory service in the army was the subject of conversation, and "militarism," to him, was the blackest of all the works of the devil; but he was bitter, and violently bitter, against the blackleg who objected to compulsory service in a Trade Union, and had spoken, times without number, in hearty encouragement of that form of siege warfare which is commonly known as a Strike. He was a pacifist of the type which seeks peace and ensues it by insisting firmly, and even to blood, that it is the other side's duty to give way.

Griselda also was a pacifist—when it suited her and when she had got her way. She believed in a future World-Amity, brought about chiefly by Woman; meanwhile, she exulted loudly and frequently in the fighting qualities of her sex. Like William, she had no quarrel with Continental nations; on the contrary, what she had seen of Continental nations during a fortnight's stay at Interlaken had inclined her to look on them with favour. Like William, her combatant instincts were concentrated on antagonists nearer home; she knew them better and therefore disliked them more. It is a mistake to suppose that either nations or individuals will necessarily like the people they see most of; if you must know a man in order to love him, you seldom hate a man with whom you have not acquaintance. Nothing could have been more ideally peaceful than the relations of China and England during the Middle Ages—for the simple reason that China and England knew absolutely nothing of each other. In the same way, if in a lesser degree, Griselda and William had a friendly feeling for Germany and the German people. They had never been to Germany and knew nothing of her history or politics; but they had heard of the Germans as intelligent people addicted to spectacles, beer and sonatas, and established on the banks of the Rhine. And—the Rhine being some way off—they liked them.

As internationalists they had no words too strong for standing armies and their methods; but upon military operations against domestic tyrants they looked with less disapproval. There existed, I believe, in the back of their minds some ill-defined distinction between bloodshed perpetrated by persons clad in uniform and by persons not so clad—between fighting with bayonets and fighting with bombs and brickbats. The one was militarism and unjustifiable; the other heroism and holy. Had you been unkind enough to pen them into a corner and force them to acknowledge that there are many born warriors out of khaki, they would have ended probably by declaring that one should take arms only against tyranny and in a righteous cause—and so have found themselves in entire agreement not only with their adversary but with the Tory Party, the German Emperor, the professional soldier and poor humanity in general. The elect, when one comes to examine them, are not always so very elect. The difficulty would have been to persuade them that there could be two opinions concerning a cause they espoused; their little vision was as narrow as it was pure, and their little minds were so seldom exhausted by thinking. Apostles of the reign of Woman and of International Amity, they might have been summed up as the perfect type of aggressor.

With regard to what used to be called culture (before August 1914), the attainments of William and Griselda were very much on a level. They read newspapers written by persons who wholly agreed with their views; they read pamphlets issued, and books recommended, by societies of which they were members. From these they quoted, in public and imposingly, with absolute faith in their statements. Of history and science, of literature and art, they knew nothing, or next to nothing; and, their ignorance being mutual, neither bored the other by straying away from the subjects in which both were interested.... As I have said, their mating was an ideal mating.

The period of their engagement was not without its beauty; an ever-present consciousness of their mission to mankind did not prevent them from being blissful as loving young couples are blissful—it merely coloured their relations and spiritualized them. One evening, not long before their wedding, they sat together in Battersea Park on a bench and dedicated their mutual lives to the service of Progress and Humanity. They had invented a suitable formula for the occasion and repeated it softly, one after the other, holding each other's hands. Griselda's voice trembled as she vowed, in semi-ecclesiastical phraseology, that not even her great love for William should wean her from her life's work; and William's voice shook back as he vowed in his turn that not even Griselda, the woman of his dreams, should make him neglectful of the call of Mankind and his duty to the holiest of causes. It was a very solemn little moment; man and woman, affianced lovers, they dedicated themselves to their mission, the uplifting of the human race. They were spared the doubts which would have assailed wiser heads as to the manner of accomplishing their mission; and as they sat side by side on the bench, with their hands clasped, they knew themselves for acceptable types and forerunners of the world they were helping to create.... Man and Woman, side by side, vowed to service.

"We shall never forget this evening," Griselda whispered as the sun dipped down in glory. "In all our lives there can be nothing more beautiful than this."

She was right; the two best gifts of life are love and an approving conscience. These twain, William and Griselda, loved each other sincerely— if not with the tempestuous passion of a Romeo and a Juliet, with an honest and healthy affection; they had for each other an attraction which could set their pulses beating and start them dreaming dreams. That evening, on the bench in Battersea Park, they had dreamed their dreams—while their consciences looked on and smiled. They foreshadowed their home not only as a nest where they two and their children should dwell, but as a centre of light and duty—as they understood duty and light; a meeting-place for the like-minded, where fresh courage could be gathered for the strife with prejudice and evil. They pictured themselves (this was in June 1914) as what they would have called Powers—as a man and a woman working for progress and destined to leave their mark. The sense of their destiny awed and elated them—and they walked away from Battersea Park with their hearts too full for speech.

On the way home a flaring headline distracted Griselda temporarily from her dreams. "Who's this Archduke that's been assassinated?" she asked. (Her morning's reading had been confined to *The Suffragette*.)

"Austrian," William informed her. (He had read the *Daily Herald*.) "Franz Joseph—no, Franz Ferdinand—the heir to the Austrian throne."

"Who assassinated him?" his betrothed inquired, not very much interested.

"I can't remember their names," William admitted, "but there seem to have been several in it. Anyhow, he's been assassinated. Somewhere in the Balkans. With bombs."

"Oh!" said Griselda, ceasing to be interested at all. Her mind had turned from traffic in strange archdukes and was running on a high resolve; the solemn vow of service was translating itself into action.

"I shall go to the meeting to-morrow," she announced, "and make my protest."

William knew what was passing in her mind and made no effort to dissuade her. No more than she dared he let their mutual happiness enervate them—it must urge them to high endeavour, to struggle and sacrifice for the Cause.

"I'll go too," he said simply, "if I can manage to get a ticket."

"Oh, I'll get you a ticket," Griselda told him; "they're sure to have some at the office"—and thanked him with a squeeze of the fingers that set his pulses beating.

She was as good as her word, and the next night saw him in a Cabinet Minister's audience. From his seat in the arena (their seats were not together and the pair had entered separately) his eye sought for Griselda and found her easily in the first row of the balcony—most obviously composed and with her gloved hands folded on the rail. She was dressed in pale blue, with a flowered toque perched on her head; her blue silk blouse, in view of possibilities, was firmly connected by safety-pins with the belt of her blue cloth skirt, and her hair secured more tightly than usual by an extra allowance of combs. Previous experience had taught her the wisdom of these measures. As usual, in accordance with the tradition of her party, she had insisted in her costume on the ultra-feminine note; her blouse savoured of Liberty and there was a cluster of rosebuds at her breast. She was breathing quickly, so her mouth was more open than usual; otherwise she gave no sign of mental or physical trepidation—save a studied indifference which might have betrayed her to an eye sufficiently acute. To William she looked adorable and his heart swelled with admiration of her courage and determination to sustain her in her protest to the uttermost; he vowed to himself to be worthy of such a mate.

He did his best to prove himself worthy when the critical moment came. He waited for that moment during more than three-quarters of an hour—for Griselda was not without confederates, and three ladies in picture hats and a gentleman in the garb of a Nonconformist minister had arisen at intervals to make the running before her voice rang out. All were suppressed, though not without excitement; two of the ladies parted with their hats and the clergyman broke a chair. The chair and the clergyman having been alike removed, the audience buzzed down into silence, and for full five minutes there was peace—until the speaker permitted himself a jesting allusion to the recently exported objectors. A man with a steward's rosette in his coat was stationed in the gangway close to William; and as the laughter the jest had provoked died away, he swore under his breath, "By God, there's another in the balcony!" William swung round, saw Griselda on her feet and heard her voice shrill out—to him an inspiration and a clarion, to the steward a source of profanity.

"Mr. Chairman, I rise to protest against the speaker's gross insult to the noble women who——"

A man in the seat behind clapped his hands on her shoulders and rammed her back into her chair—where she writhed vigorously, calling him coward and demanding how he dared! His grip, sufficiently hard to be unpleasant, roused her fighting instincts and gave a fillip to her conscientious protest; in contact with actual, if not painful, personal violence, she found it easier to scream, hit out and struggle. Two stewards, starting from either end of the row of chairs, were wedging themselves towards her; she clung to her seat with fingers and toes, and shrieked a regulation formula which the meeting drowned in opprobrium. Conscious of rectitude, the jeers and hoots but encouraged her and fired her blood; and when her hands were wrenched from their hold on the chair she clung and clawed to the shoulder of her next-door neighbour—a stout and orthodox Liberal who thrust her from him, snorting indignation. One steward had her gripped under the armpits, the other with difficulty mastered her active ankles; and, wriggling like a blue silk eel and crowing her indefatigable protest, she was bundled in rapid and business-like fashion to a side entrance of the building.

"Cowards!" she ejaculated as she found her feet on the pavement.

"Damned little cat!" was the ungentlemanly rejoinder. "If you come here again I'll pare your nasty little nails for you."

And, dabbing a scored left hand with his handkerchief, the steward returned to his duties—leaving Griselda in the centre of a jocular crowd attracted to the spot by several previous ejections. She was minus her rosebuds, her toque and quite half of her hairpins; on the other hand, she held tightly grasped in her fingers a crumpled silk necktie which had once been the property of a stout and orthodox Liberal. She was conscious that she had acted with perfect dignity as well as with unusual courage—and that consciousness, combined with her experience of similar situations, enabled her to sustain with calm contempt the attentions of the jocular crowd.

"You'd like a taxi, I suppose, miss?" the constable on duty suggested—having also considerable experience of similar situations. Griselda assented and the taxi was duly hailed. Before it arrived at the kerb she was joined on the pavement by her lover, who had left the meeting by the same door as his betrothed and in much the same manner and condition; he had parted with a shoe as well as a hat, and one of his braces was broken. A hearty shove assisted him down the steps to the pavement where, to the applause of the unthinking multitude, he fell on his knees in an attitude of adoration before Griselda's friend the constable. Recovering his equilibrium, he would have turned again to the assault; but his game attempt to re-enter the building was frustrated not only by a solidly extended arm of the law but by the intervention of Griselda herself.

"You have done enough for to-night, dear," she whispered, taking his arm. "My instructions are not to insist on arrest. We have made our protest—we can afford to withdraw."

She led the retreat to the taxi with a dignity born of practice; William, now conscious of his snapped brace, following with less deportment. The vehicle once clear of the jeering crowd, Griselda put her arms round her lover and kissed his forehead solemnly.

"My dear one," she said, "I am proud of you."

"Oh, Griselda, I'm proud of you," he murmured between their kisses. "How brave you are—how wonderful!—how dared they! ... I went nearly mad when I saw them handling you—I hit out, and the cowards knocked me down.... A woman raising her voice on the side of justice—and they silence her with brutal violence——"

"It's only what we must expect, dear," she whispered back, stroking his rumpled hair. "Remember this is War—God knows it's horrible, but we must not shrink from it."

She spoke from her heart, from the profound ignorance of the unread and unimaginative ... and once more in the darkness of the taxi the warriors clasped and kissed.

CHAPTER III

After the usual hesitations and excursions they had settled on their future home—a tiny flat in Bloomsbury, central and handy for the perpetual getting about to meetings which was so integral a part of their well-filled, bustling lives. They furnished it lovingly and with what they considered good taste; Griselda brought in her friends to admire, and engaged a respectable woman who was to "do" for them and have all in readiness when they returned from their four weeks' honeymoon—and they were as foolishly happy over their nest as any other loving little couple.

They were married towards the end of July—to be exact, on the twenty-third day of the month. The wedding took place in Balham from the house of Griselda's aunt; the ceremony was performed by an enlightened vicar who had consented to omit the ignoble vow of obedience; and the church was thronged to its doors with comrades and ardent sympathizers. The advanced Press spread itself over the description of the ceremony and—in view of the fact that the bridesmaids, six in number, had all done time for assault—even the Press that was not advanced considered the event worth a paragraph. The pair were snapshotted on leaving the church with the customary direful results, and the modest residence of Griselda's aunt could hardly accommodate the flood of progressive guests. There was rice and slipper-throwing and a whirl of good wishes—and Griselda, flushed, looked pretty, and in William's eyes quite lovely.

They left by an afternoon train for Dover and crossed the next day to Ostend.

Their selection of the Belgian Ardennes for a honeymoon was due to Griselda's long-standing acquaintance with a cosmopolitan female revolutionist understood to be of Russian Polish extraction. Owing, it was further understood, to her pronounced opinions and pronounced manner of expressing them, she had long ceased to be welcome in the land that gave her birth; at any rate, she avoided it studiously and existed chiefly at a series of epoch-making revolutionary meetings which she addressed by turns in bad German, worse French, and worst English. She wrote vehement pamphlets in all these languages and prided herself on the fact that, on the Continent at least, they were frequently suppressed by the police; wore tartan blouses, a perennial smile, and a hat that was always askew. For some reason or another she was the possessor of a cottage in the heart of the Belgian Ardennes—which she visited on the rare occasions when she was not plying her epoch-making activities in London, Vienna, or New York. A week once a year was about all the use she made of it—reappearing after her seven days' seclusion with a brace of new pamphlets burning for the Press, and like a giant refreshed for the fight. This estimable woman was as good-natured as she was revolutionary, and hearing that Griselda was thinking of a rural honeymoon, she hastened to offer the happy couple the loan of her Belgian property, which was as secluded as heart could desire. Griselda, since her fortnight at Interlaken, had hankered for another stay abroad; she jumped at the offer, and William—whose acquaintance with foreign parts was limited to an International Socialist Congress in Holland—-jumped gladly in unison with her. Madame Amberg beamed with joy at their delighted acceptance of her offer; she kissed Griselda, shook hands with William and promised to make all the necessary arrangements for their stay—to write to the old woman who looked after the cottage and tell her when to expect them. She babbled rhapsodically of honeymoons and the joys of the Forest of Arden—forgetting how bored she was in the Forest of Arden at the end of a seven-days' stay there—and further directed them how to reach it, looked out trains and suggested hotels.

Heaven smiled on the opening of their married life; Dover was a receding beauty in the distance and the Channel a good-natured lake. As their boat chunked between the long piers of Ostend they held and squeezed each other's hands ecstatically, the crowd collecting on the gangway side enabling them to do so unnoticed. The consciousness of their total ignorance of the language of the country gave them an agitated moment as they set foot on foreign soil—but, taken in tow by a polyglot porter, they were safely transferred from the quay to a second-class carriage, with instructions to change at Brussels; and, having changed obediently, were in due course set down at Namur. Madame Amberg had advised them to lodge with economy at the Hotel de Hollande near the station; but another specimen of the polyglot porter pounced down and annexed them firmly for his own more distant establishment, and after a feeble resistance they followed him meekly and were thrust with their bags into the omnibus lying in wait for them. They felt it their duty as the vehicle rattled them along to make a few depreciatory and high-principled remarks on the subject of the towering fortifications; but having thus satisfied their consciences they relapsed into mere enjoyment of rest, novelty, a good dinner, and a view of the lazy Meuse. After dinner, when the fortress above them was fading into the soft blackness of a warm summer night, they walked arm-in-arm by the river and were quite unutterably happy.

They rose early in the morning to catch the little river boat for Dinant; caught it with the aid of their guardian, the porter, and camped side by side on its deck to enjoy the sauntering trip. They enjoyed it so much and engrossingly that for the space of a morning they forgot their high principles, they forgot even Woman and Democracy; they were tourists only, agape and delighted, with their green Cook's tickets in their pockets. Yet, after all, they were something more than tourists; they were young man and woman who loved each other tenderly and whose happy lives were in tune with the happy landscape. Often they forgot to look at the happy landscape for the joy of gazing into each other's dear blue eyes.

The boat puffed finally to Dinant, where they stayed the night as planned; where they stared at the cupola'd church and the cliffs, walked to the split rock on the road to Anseremme, and bought some of the gingerbread their guide-book had told them to buy. They ate it next day, with no particular approval, on the final stage of their journey, in a train that puffed and pottered between heights and orchards in the winding company of a stream. It puffed and pottered them at last to their wayside destination—where a smiling and loutish country boy slouched up to take possession of them and their modest baggage. They understood not a word of his thick-throated patois, but knew from information imparted beforehand by Madame Amberg that this was their housekeeper's grandson and deputed to serve as their guide. He gripped a bag easily in either hand, and led the way past the few small houses ranged neatly as a miniature village alongside the miniature station—and so by the white road that kept the river company. After a mile or thereabout they left the white road, turning sharply to the right at a cleft in the riverside cliff and striking a cart-track, scarcely more than a path, into a valley twisted back among the hills.

It was a valley the like of which they had never seen, which the world seemed to have forgotten; a cool green vision of summer and solitary peace. Water had cleft in the table-land above them a passage that time had made leafy and gracious and laid aside for their finding. Through the flat, lush pastures that divided the bold slopes there looped and tangled a tiny brook on its way to the Meuse and the sea, a winding ribbon of shadow, of shimmer and reflection. Up the slopes rising steeply from the pastures there clustered tree above tree—so thickly set that where the valley dwindled in the distance they might have been moss on the hill-side. There was no one in sight and no sound but their footsteps and the birds; it was all a green prettiness given over to birds and themselves.

"Isn't it wonderful?" Griselda said, not knowing that her voice had dropped and lost its shrillness. "I never thought there could be such a place."

She spoke the truth, if in hackneyed and unthinking phrase; in her busy and crowded little mind, the reflection of her busy little life, there had been no room for visions of a deep and solitary peace. Involuntarily, as they walked they drew nearer together and went closely side by side; the sweet aloofness of the valley not only amazed them, it awed them; they were dimly conscious of being in contact with something which in its silent, gracious way was disquieting as well as beautiful. Their theory and practice of life, so far, was the theory and practice of their purely urban environment, of crowds, committees and grievances and cocksure little people like themselves—and lo, out of an atmosphere of cocksureness and hustle they had stepped, as it seemed without warning, into one of mystery and the endless patience of the earth. Out here, in this strange overpowering peace, it was difficult to be conscious of grievances political or ethical; instead came a new, undefined and uneasy sense of personal inadequacy and shrinkage, a sense of the unknown and hitherto unallowed-for, a fear of something undreamed of in their rabid and second-hand philosophy.... Not that they reasoned after this fashion, or were capable of analysing the source of the tremor that mingled with their physical pleasure, their sheer delight of the eye; but before they had been in the valley many hours they sympathized in secret (they did not know why) with Madame Amberg's consistent avoidance of its loveliness, saw hazily and without comprehension why, for all her praise of its beauties, she was so loth to dwell there. The place, though they knew it not, was a New Idea to them—and therefore a shadow of terror to their patterned and settled convictions. As such their organized and regulated minds shrank from it at once and instinctively—cautiously apprehensive lest the New Idea should tamper with accepted beliefs, disturb established views and call generally for the exercise of faculties hitherto unused. They had an uneasy foreboding—never mentioned aloud by either, though troublous to both—that long contact with solitude and beauty might end by confusing issues that once were plain, and so unfitting them for the work of Progress and Humanity—for committees, agitations, the absorbing of pamphlets and the general duty of rearranging the universe.

There was something, probably, in the frame of mind in which they approached the valley; they came of a migratory, holiday race, and had seen green beauty before, if only fleetingly and at intervals. What they had lacked before was the insight into beauty born of their own hearts' content, the wonder created by their own most happy love.... They followed their guide for the most part in silence, relieved that he had ceased his well-meaning attempts to make them understand his jargon, and speaking, when they spoke at all, in voices lowered almost to a whisper.

"What's that?" Griselda queried, still under her breath. "That" was a flash of blue fire ahead of them darting slantwise over the stream. Later they learned to understand that a flash of blue fire meant kingfisher; but for the moment William shook his head, nonplussed, and hazarded only, "It's a bird."

For half-an-hour or so it was only the birds and themselves; then at a turn in the narrowing valley they came in sight of cows nuzzling the pastures. Several cows, parti-coloured black and white like the cows of a Noah's Ark; and, further on, a tiny farm house standing close up to the trees in its patch of vegetable garden. They knew from Madame Amberg of the existence of the tiny farmhouse; it was an old woman living there who would "do" for them during their stay at the neighbouring cottage—cook and clean and make tidy in return for a moderate wage. The barking of a kennelled nondescript brought the old woman shuffling to the door—to welcome them (presumably) in her native tongue and to take their measure from head to heel with a pair of shrewd, sunken eyes. Of her verbal greetings they understood nothing but the mention of Madame Amberg; but, having looked them up and down enough, the old lady shuffled back into her kitchen for the key of the revolutionist's property. She reappeared with the key in one hand and a copper stewpan in the other—wherewith she waved the signal to advance, and shuffled off in guidance, ahead of her grandson and the visitors. A quarter of an hour's more walking on a dwindling path brought them in sight of their sylvan honeymoon abode; it had originally been built for the use of a woodman, and was a four-roomed cottage on the edge of the wood overlooking the stream and the pasture of the black-and-white cows. Madame Peys (they knew at least her name) unlocked the door and ushered them into the kitchen, where the boy deposited their bags.

CHAPTER IV

The cottage was what any one who know Madame Amberg might have expected her cottage to be. It was sparsely furnished, except with explosive literature; there were very few chairs, and those few verging on decrepitude, but numerous tracts and pamphlets in divers civilized languages. Kitchen utensils were conspicuous chiefly by their absence, and presumably the owner relied consistently on the loan of the copper stewpan which had accompanied her guests from the farm. On the other hand, the kitchen walls were adorned by photographs, more or less fly-blown, of various political extremists, and a signed presentment of Rosa Luxemburg adorned a bedroom mantelpiece.

While Madame Peys made play with the stew-pan and a kettle, the honeymoon couple unpacked their bags and examined their new domain: still, to a certain extent, overawed by the silence and loneliness around it; still, unknown to themselves, speaking more gently and with more hesitation than usual. It was the familiar tang of the books and pamphlets, with which the shelves were crammed and the floor was heaped, that first revived their quieted spirits and created a sense of home. Woman and Democracy, even on the backs of books, had power to act as a tonic and trumpet-call, to reflect the atmosphere of noise and controversy where alone they could breathe with comfort. With unconscious relief they turned from the window and the prospect of the valley, green and untenanted, to entrench themselves against the assaults of the unknown behind the friendly and familiar volumes that had overflowed from Madame Amberg's deal book-shelves to Madame Amberg's uncarpeted floor. Conning them, handling them and turning their pages, they were again on the solid ground of impatient intolerance; they were back amongst their own, their cherished certainties. William in the presence of Belfort Bax felt his feet once more beneath him; Griselda, recognizing a pamphlet by Christabel Pankhurst, ceased to be troubled by the loneliness around her, grew animated and raised her voice.... And the savoury mess which Madame produced from her stewpan, combined with the no less excellent coffee that followed, dispelled for the moment the sense of mystery and the shadow of the New Idea.

The shadow obtruded itself more than once during the next three weeks or so; but on the whole they managed with fair success to be in the country and not of it—to create in the heart of their immemorial valley a little refuge and atmosphere of truly advanced suburbia. Their existence in the Ardennes valley was one of mutual affection and study—by which latter term they understood principally the reading of books they agreed with. From the cares and worries of housekeeping they were blissfully and entirely free; Madame Peys did their catering, taking toll, no doubt, of their simplicity and ignorance of French, but taking it with tact and discretion. Her bills were a weekly trouble to Griselda but not on account of their length; what she disliked was the embarrassing moment when she strove to conceal her complete ignorance of the items and difficulty in grasping the total as set forth in un-English-looking ciphers. Their tidying was also done daily and adequately, their cooking more than adequately; Madame Peys called them in the morning, set the house to rights and their various meals going, and looked in at intervals during the day, departing for the last time when supper was cooked and laid. Their daily doings fell naturally into routine; they rose of a morning to coffee steaming on the stove; and, having digested their breakfast, they usually proceeded to walk a little, concluding the exercise by sitting under the trees with a book which William read aloud to Griselda. They lunched sometimes in picnic fashion, sometimes at home; in the afternoon took another stroll or sat at home reading, with happy little interludes of talk. On two or three days they made small excursions to one of the neighbouring villages; on others William, with a pen and a frown of importance, would establish himself at the table after lunch was cleared away; he had a tract in hand on the Woman Question, and Griselda gently but firmly insisted that even in the first ecstasy of their honeymoon he should not lay it aside. Having a due sense of the value of his epoch-making work, he did not require much pressing; and while he frowned and scribbled and frowned and paused, she would sit by reading, and now and again glance up that she might meet his eye and smile. Long afterwards, months afterwards, when he had forgotten the epoch-making work and all he had meant to prove by it, he would remember how she had risen and come behind him, smoothing and fondling his ruffled hair and bending over to kiss him. He would drop his pen and lift his face to hers, sometimes in silence and sometimes murmuring foolishness.

In time, as the peaceful days crept by, they were sorry that, yielding to a romantic impulse, they had directed that neither paper nor letter should be forwarded during their absence. As a result of this prohibition their entire correspondence while they stayed in the valley consisted of one picture-postcard despatched by Madame Amberg from Liverpool at the moment of her embarkation for an extended lecture tour in the States. It was sent three days after their wedding, and expressed exuberant affection, but was singularly lacking in news of the outside world. To remove the prohibition would be to confess failure and suggest boredom, therefore neither ventured to hint at it; all the same, they knew in their secret hearts that they had overrated their resourcefulness. It was not that they palled on each other—far from it; but part at least of their mutual attraction was their mutual interest in certain subjects and limited phases of activity. Madame Amberg's revolutionary library, valuable as it was in distracting their thoughts from the silence and beauty around them and defending them against the unknown, could not entirely supply the place of daily whirl and unceasing snarl and argument; William pined unconsciously for the din and dust of the platform and Griselda missed the weekly temper into which she worked herself in sympathy with her weekly *Suffragette*. She missed it so much that at last she was moved to utterance—late on a still, heavy evening in August, when once or twice there had come up the valley a distant mutter as of thunder.

"Dear," she said gently, as they sat by the window after supper, "I don't know how you feel about it, but I am beginning to think that our life here is almost too peaceful. It is beautiful to sit here together and dream and forget the world—but is it a preparation for the life we are to lead? Is it a preparation for our work?"

William sighed a gentle sigh of relief, and his hand went out to his wife's in a squeeze of agreement and gratitude. As usual, their minds had jumped together and the thought of twain had been uttered by the lips of one.

"I've been thinking the same thing myself," he said. "It has struck me more than once. As you say, it's beautiful here in the heart of the country—nothing could be more beautiful. But I have wondered, especially lately, if it isn't enervating. It is good for some people, perhaps; but when you have an aim in life and the fighting spirit in you——"

"Yes," Griselda flared responsively, "it's the fighting spirit—and the Cause calling to us. I've been hearing the call getting louder and louder; we can't stand aside any longer, we haven't the right to stand aside. How can I—how dare I—rest and enjoy myself when, there are noble women struggling for freedom, suffering for freedom, keeping the flag flying——?"

And the unconscious little humbug clasped her hands and, from force of habit, rose to her feet, addressing an imaginary audience. William, an equally unconscious humbug, also rose to his feet and kissed her. It was one of those happy and right-minded moments in which inclination agrees with duty, and they were able to admire themselves and each other for a sacrifice which had cost them nothing.

The decision taken, there remained only the details of their speedy departure to settle. Their first impatient impulse was to leave for Brussels on the morrow, but on consideration they decided that the morrow would be too soon. Investigation of a local time-table revealed the fact that the connection with Brussels—the only tolerable connection—meant a start in the very early morning; but an early start meant an overnight warning to the farm-boy, Philippe, that his services would be needful to carry their bags to the station—and the farm-people, all of them, went to bed soon after the sun and were certainly by now asleep. There was, further, the old lady to settle with where financial matters were concerned, and it always took time to make out her illegible bill. On reflection, therefore, they decided for the following day.

"I hope," Griselda meditated, "that I shall be able to make Madame Peys understand that we want the boy the first thing in the morning. I expect she will see what I mean if I show her the train in the time-table and say 'Philippe,' and point to the bags. That ought to make it clear. It rather detracts from the enjoyment of being abroad—not being able to make people understand what you say. Interlaken was much more convenient in that way; all the waiters spoke English quite nicely. And the understanding is even more difficult than the speaking. To-night Madame was talking away hard to me all the time she was cooking our supper, but I couldn't make out one word she said—only that she was very excited. I said, 'Oui, oui,' every now and then, because she seemed to expect it, and I was sorry to see her upset. I thought perhaps one of the people at the farm was ill, but I've seen her son and his wife and the boy since, so it can't be that. Of course, she may have other relations in some other part of the country—or perhaps something has happened to one of the cows. I could see she was worried."

They sat until late side by side by the open window and talked in snatches of the world they were going back to—the dear, familiar, self-important world of the agitated and advanced. Its dust was already in their nostrils, its clamour already in their ears; in three days more they would be in it once again with their own little turbulent folk. The mere thought increased their sense of their own value, and they grew gay and excited as they talked and planned, instinctively turning their backs on the window and shutting out sight and sound of the country peace, the oppressive peace in which they had no part.

"What shall we do to-morrow, darling?" Griselda asked at length. The question was prompted by her longing for to-morrow to be over and her mind was in search of some method for inducing it to pass with swiftness.

They considered the point with that object in view, and decided that should the day prove fine they would spend it away from the cottage, taking their lunch with them. There was a winding path leading up through the woods to the heights which they had not yet explored except for a short distance; they would start out, provisioned, soon after breakfast, to go where the path led them, and eat their meal on the hill-top. Then home to supper, settlement with Madame, and an early departure next morning.... So they planned comfortably and without misgiving, while the world seethed in the melting-pot and the Kaiser battered at Liège.

"If it's fine," William cautioned again as they mounted the stairs to bed. "I've heard thunder several times in the distance, so we may have a storm in the morning."

There was no storm or sign of a storm in the morning. It must have passed over, Griselda said; she had listened to its faint and distant mutterings for half-an-hour before she fell asleep. Their meal of coffee and new-laid eggs was waiting on the stove as usual, and Madame Peys had vanished as usual before they came down to partake of it. They hard-boiled more eggs while they breakfasted, and, the meal disposed of, set to work to cut plentiful sandwiches and otherwise furnish their basket. As their road up the hill did not lead them past the farm, and Madame Peys had not yet put in an appearance for the process of tidying up, William inscribed in large round-hand on an envelope the word "*Sorti*," as a sign to their housekeeper that the preparation of a midday meal was unnecessary; and having placed the announcement on the kitchen table, duly weighted with a saucer, he took the basket on one arm, his wife on the other, and set out.

They met not a soul that morning as they mounted the winding little path—somewhat slowly, for the winding little path was not only longer than they had expected but very steep in places. Further, the day was hot even under the trees, and they rested more than once before they reached their goal, the heights that crowned the valley; rested with their backs against a beech-trunk, and talked of themselves and what interested them — of meetings past and to come, of the treachery of the Labour Party, of the wickedness of the Government and the necessity for terrifying its members by new and astounding tactics. The idea had been to lunch when the heights above them were gained; but the weight of the basket made itself felt in the heat, and they were still some distance from their goal when they decided it was time to lighten it. They did so in the customary fashion, ate well and heartily, and although they allowed an unhurried interval for digestion were even less enthusiastic about their uphill walk than they had been before partaking of lunch. It was a relief to them when at last they emerged from the trees and found themselves high above the valley and entering on a wide stretch of upland; the wide stretch of upland had no particular attraction, but it denoted the limits of their excursion and a consequent return downhill.

"Don't you think we've about been far enough?" Griselda suggested. "There's rather a glare now we're out of the wood, and it's not particularly pretty here."

William agreed whole-heartedly—adding, however, as a rider, that a rest was desirable before they started homeward, and that if they went as far as the rise in the ground a hundred yards to their right they would probably have quite a good view, and he expected there would be a nice breeze. In accordance with these expectations they mounted the knoll, found the breeze and the view they expected, and subsided in the shade of a bush. If they had but known it, they were the last tourists of their race who for many and many a day to come were to look on the scene before them. Had they but known it, they would certainly have scanned it more keenly; as it was, they surveyed the wide landscape contentedly, but with no particular enthusiasm. On every side of them were the rounded uplands—a table-land gently swelling and cleft here and there by wooded valleys. On their right was the deep cleft from which they had mounted through the woods; and before them the ground dropped sharply to the edge of a cliff, the boundary of a wider cleft running at right angles to their own green valley of silence. It was along this wider cleft that the railway ran, the little branch line that to-morrow (so they thought) was to take them on the first stage of their journey. From their perch on the hill-top they could see the three ribbons of dark track, white road and shadowed river which between them filled the valley. The wall of rock jutted forward on their left, hiding, as they knew, the wayside railway station at which they had arrived and the cluster of neat houses beside it; to the right again there was a bend no less sharp—and between the two a stretch of empty road.

"It's very pretty," said Griselda, yawning and fanning herself, "but I wish it wasn't quite so hot. I suppose there's nothing left to drink?"

William was sorry there wasn't—they had finished the last drop at lunch. Griselda sighed, stretched herself out on her elbow, with her face towards the eastern bluff, and saw coming round it a group of three or four horsemen—little toy-like horses, carrying little toy men past trees that looked like bushes. They were moving quickly; the toy-like horses were cantering on the white ribbon of road. Griselda pointed them out to William, and the pair leaned forward to watch them pass, hundreds of feet below.

"They're scampering along," she said; "they must be in a hurry. What funny little things they look from here—like insects! They'll be out of sight in a minute—no, they've stopped.... I believe they're turning back."

The funny little things had halted simultaneously at the foot of the jutting cliff which hid the village and the station from the eyes of William and Griselda. As Griselda had said, in another moment they would have been round it and out of sight, and fifty more yards or so beyond the bend would have brought them to the outskirts of the village. Instead, they halted and drew together for an instant; then one funny little thing, detaching himself from the group, scampered backwards by the road he had come, and continued scampering till he rounded the eastward bluff. His insects of companions remained grouped where he had left them, their horses shifting backwards and forwards on the white surface of the road.

"They're waiting for him to come back," Griselda concluded idly, "I expect they've forgotten something."

What they had forgotten proved to be a column of horsemen curving in swift and orderly fashion round the foot of the eastward bluff. It came on, a supple and decorative line, bending with the bend and straightening as the valley straightened.

"Soldiers," said William, with the orthodox accent of contempt—following with a pleasure he would not for worlds have admitted the sinuous windings of the troop. There is in the orderly movement of men an attraction which few can resist; it appealed even to his elementary sense of the rhythmic, and he, like Griselda, bent forward to watch and to listen to the distant clatter of hoofs echoed back from the walls of the valley. As the horsemen swung out of sight round the westward bluff and the clatter of hoof-beats deadened, he held up a finger, and Griselda asked, "What is it?"

"Guns," he said. "Cannon—don't you hear them?"

She did; a soft, not unpleasing thud, repeated again and again, and coming down the breeze from the northward.

"It must be manoeuvres," he explained. "That's what those soldiers are doing. I expect it's what they call the autumn manoeuvres."

"Playing at murder," Griselda commented, producing the orthodox sigh. She had heard the phrase used by a pacifist orator in the Park and considered it apt and telling. "What a waste of time—and what a brutalizing influence on the soldiers themselves! Ah, if only women had a say in national affairs!" ... and she made the customary glib oration on her loved and familiar text. Before it was quite finished, William held up his finger again—needlessly, for Griselda had stopped short on her own initiative. This time it was a crackle of sharp little shots, not far away and softened like the sound of the heavier guns, but comparatively close at hand and, if their ears did not deceive them, just beyond the westward bluff.

"They're pretending to fight in the village," Griselda said. "How silly! Firing off guns and making believe to shoot people."

"Militarism," William assented, "is always silly." And he, in his turn, enlarged on his favourite text, the impossibility of international warfare, owing to the ever-growing solidarity of the European working-classes— his little homily being punctuated here and there by a further crackle from below. When he had enlarged sufficiently and Griselda had duly agreed, he returned as it were to private life and suggested:

"If you're feeling more rested, shall we make a start? It's cooler under the trees."

They started, accordingly, on their homeward way, which was even longer than the route they had taken in the morning: one little wood path was very like another and they managed to take a wrong turning, bear too much to the right and make a considerable detour. When the cottage came in sight they were both thirsty, and secretly relieved that their last excursion was over.

"We'll put on the spirit-lamp and have some tea," Griselda announced as they pushed open the door. "Oh dear! it's lovely to think we shall be in London so soon. How I would love a strawberry ice! Where's the match-box?"

It was not until the match-box was found and the spirit-lamp kindled that William discovered on the kitchen table a mystery in the shape of a document. It was an unimposing looking document, not over clean, indicted in pencil on the reverse of the half-sheet of paper on which William that morning had written his announcement of "*Sorti.*" Like William's announcement, the communication was in French, of a kind—presumably uneducated French if one judged by the writing; and like William the author of the communication (in all likelihood Madame Peys) had placed it in the centre of the table and crowned it with a saucer before leaving.

"I suppose it must be for us," William remarked doubtfully. "I can't make out a word of it—can you?"

"Of course not," Griselda returned with a spice of irritation—she was tired and her boots hurt her. "I couldn't read that ridiculous writing if it was English. It's that silly old woman, Madame Peys, I suppose; but what is the good of her writing us letters when she knows we can't read them?"

"Perhaps," William suggested, "it's to say she won't be able to cook our supper to-night?"

"Very likely," his wife agreed, the spice of irritation still more pronounced. "If that's it, we shall have to do with eggs—we used up the cold meat for sandwiches at lunch, and there's nothing else in the house. We'd better go round to the farm when we've had our tea and find out what she wants—stupid old thing! Whether she comes here or not, we must see her to get the bill and order the boy for the morning. But I don't mean to move another step till I've had my tea."

CHAPTER V

They had their tea, Griselda with her boots off and her aching feet resting on a chair; and after she had lapped up two comfortable cups her irritation subsided and she was once again her pleasant and chattering little self. William, to give her a further rest, volunteered, though with some hesitation, to make the visit to the farm alone; in his mind, as in her own, Griselda was the French scholar of the pair, a reputation due to the fact that it was she to whom Madame Peys preferred, as a rule, to address her unintelligible remarks. Griselda knew what the offer cost him and generously declined to take advantage of it—stipulating only for a few minutes more repose before encasing her weary feet again in boots. The few minutes drew out into half-an-hour or more, and the shadows were lengthening in the valley when they started on their walk to the farm. They started arm-in-arm, the wife leaning on the husband; but when they came in sight of the house Griselda took her arm from William's and they drew a little apart.

They need not have troubled to observe the minor proprieties; not a soul stirred, not a nose showed itself as they opened the little wooden gate of the garden and made for the open door. They were both of them unobservant of country sights and sounds, and it was not until they had knocked in vain on the open door and called in vain on the name of Madame Peys that they were struck by the absence of the usual noises of the farm. There was neither lowing of cows nor crowing and clucking of poultry; and the nondescript of a dog who usually heralded the approach of a visitor by strangling tugs at his chain and vociferous canine curses, for once had allowed their advent to pass unchallenged. They realized suddenly that there was a strange silence from the kennel and turned simultaneously to look at it.

"It's odd," said William. "I suppose they've all gone out, and taken the dog with them."

"Where are the cocks and hens?" said Griselda suddenly. As if in answer to her query, a scraggy pullet at the awkward age appeared on the top of the farmyard gate, flapped groundwards and proceeded to investigate the neighbouring soil with a series of businesslike pecks. Their eyes turned towards the yard whence the pullet had emerged in search of her usual bevy of feathered companions; but the satisfied cluck of the bird as she sampled a seed remained unechoed and unanswered and brought no comrade to the spot. Obviously the family excursion was unlikely to be accompanied by a lengthy procession of poultry; and moved by a common impulse of wonder William and Griselda made for the gate and surveyed the farmyard beyond ... The doors of byre and stable were standing wide, untenanted either by horse or by cow, and the two farm-carts had vanished. There was a small dark square in the corner of the yard marking the spot where yesterday an imprisoned mother had kept watch and ward over a baker's dozen of attractive yellow downlings; now the dark square was the only trace of mother, chicks and cell.

"I wish," said William, "that we could read what's written on that paper. What can have happened to them all?"

"What's happened to them is that they've gone," Griselda returned with decision. "And gone for a good long time—people don't take their cows and chickens and cart-horses with them when they go for a week-end. I suppose they're moving and taking another farm."

"Ye-es?" William agreed doubtfully. "But I shouldn't have thought they'd have moved at such short notice—with all those animals. Of course, if they're moving, they'll come back for what they've left—those spades and the wheelbarrow and the furniture. There are a lot of things still in the kitchen ... they may come to fetch them to-night."

"They're sure to," his wife said hopefully. "Besides, Madame Peys would never leave us without milk or provisions for the morning—she's much too considerate. I daresay the new farm isn't far off, and she'll either come herself or send Philippe. Then we must explain about the train to-morrow morning."

William, still doubtful in spite of Griselda's optimism, paused at the half-open door of the kitchen, pushed it more widely ajar and surveyed the interior in detail.

"They must have started in rather a hurry," he commented.

The comment was justified by the disordered appearance of the room, suggesting a departure anything but leisurely and packing anything but methodical. There was an arm-chair upturned by the hearth where the ashes of the wood fire still glowed and reddened in places, but all the other chairs had vanished. The heavy table was still in the centre of the room, but a smaller one had gone, and several pans were missing from the row that shimmered on the wall opposite the fireplace. The canary's cage and the clock on the mantelpiece had departed; and the china cupboard standing wide open was rifled of part of its contents—apparently a random selection.

On the floor in one corner was a large chequered table-cloth knotted into a bundle and containing, judging by its bulges, a collection of domestic objects of every shape known to the housewife. It lay discarded at the foot of the stairs like a bursting and badly cooked pudding; its formidable size and unwieldy contour accounting in themselves for the household's decision to abandon it ... There was about the place—as in all dismantled or partially dismantled rooms—an indefinite suggestion of melancholy; William and Griselda were conscious of its influence as they stood in the centre of the kitchen which they had hitherto known only as a model of orderly arrangement.

"I wonder how long they will be," Griselda said, as she and her husband came out into the dying sunlight. "It isn't any good hanging about here; if nobody has turned up we can stroll down again after supper ... I wonder if I could make an omelette—I've often watched her do it, and it doesn't seem so very difficult. How lonely that chicken looks poking about by itself."

Her eye followed the gawky pullet as it clucked and pecked in its loneliness about the vegetable garden—and suddenly her hand shot out and caught at her husband's arm.

"William," she said in a queer little whisper, "what's that?"

"What?" William queried, half-startled by the clutch and the whisper.

"Don't you see?—that heap ... beyond the gooseberry bushes!"

He looked where she pointed, and she felt him thrill, as she herself had thrilled when her hand went out to his arm; neither spoke as they went towards the end of the garden, instinctively hushing their footsteps ... The soft earth beyond the gooseberry bushes had been heaped into a long mound, and the solitary pullet was clucking and pecking at the side of a new-made grave.

They stood looking down at it in silence—dumb and uneasily fearful in the presence of a mystery beyond their powers of fathoming. The empty, untidy house behind them was suddenly a threat and a shadow; so was the loneliness and all-enclosing silence of the valley ... The damp garden earth was still fresh and black from its turning; whoever lay under it could have lain but an hour or two; and, lest the unmistakable shape of the mound should fail to indicate what it covered, some one had laid on it a red spray torn from a rose-bush and with a stick and a knot of string had fashioned a cross for the head. Two crossed hazel shoots and a handful of roses betokened that a spirit had returned to the God Who gave it.

As they stood at the graveside in the peace of the evening, the constant mutter of distant guns sent a low-spoken threat along the valley; but they were too much engrossed in their thoughts and surroundings to give it ear or heed, and it was the pullet who roused them from their stupor of dumb astonishment. Encouraged by their stillness, she drew near, surveyed the mound and with a flap of her clipped wings alighted under the cross. William instinctively bent forward to "shoo" her away, and as she fled protesting to a safer neighbourhood the husband and wife for the first time moved and spoke.

"What can have happened?" Griselda whispered. "Do you think— — William, you don't think there has been a murder?"

William shook his head, though not with excess of confidence. "There's the cross," he objected, "and the roses. A murderer would hardly put roses— —"

"I don't know," Griselda whispered back. "You hear of criminals doing such strange things—and perhaps it was done hastily, in a quarrel, and the murderer repented at once.... For all we know that paper on our kitchen table may be a confession.... I wonder whose grave it is—if it's one of the Peys. It's so odd their all having gone—there must be something wrong.... You don't suppose they've gone off to hide themselves?"

William reminded her of the absence of the farm-yard stock—and she admitted that a family seeking to elude justice would hardly be so foolish as to attempt to conceal itself from the police in the company of seven cows, two cart-horses and an entire colony of poultry. Nor, when untrodden woods lay around them, would they call attention to the crime by placing the grave of their victim in a prominent position in the garden; while it was difficult to think of the Peys family, as they had known them, as murderers and accomplices of murderers: the old lady so cheery and shrewd, her son and his wife so unintelligibly friendly, and Philippe so loutishly good-natured.

For a while a gruesome fascination held them to the side of the grave— and then Griselda quivered and said suddenly, "Let's go home." They walked away softly and closed the gate softly behind them; and, once they were well beyond it, instinctively quickened their footsteps. They walked arm-in-arm, speaking little, on their way back to the cottage, and it was not until they were almost on the threshold of their solitary homestead that it struck them that perhaps they would only be fulfilling their legal duty by informing the local authorities of the presence of the new-made grave. They discussed the idea, considered it, and after discussion rejected it: for one thing, there was the language difficulty, for another the natural shrinking of the foreigner from entangling himself in unknown processes of law—involving possible detention for the purpose of giving evidence. They decided that it would be better for the present to await events, and hope for the return of some member of the vanished family.

In after days, when after events had given him a clue, William framed his solution to the mystery of the grave and the empty farmhouse—a solution which perhaps was not correct as to detail but was certainly right in substance. Some fleeing Belgian, wounded to death, had found strength to outrun or outride the Uhlan, and seeking a refuge in the hidden valley had brought his news to the farmhouse, and died after giving it utterance. Those who heard it had buried him in haste, and straightway fled from the invader—fled clumsily, with horse and cart and cattle, leaving their scribbled, unreadable warning to the absent tenants of the cottage. Whether they fled far and successfully, or whether they were overtaken and in due course held fast behind the barrier of flesh and iron that shut off the German and his conquests from the rest of the civilized world—that William and Griselda never knew.

In the meantime, unfurnished with any clue, unknowing of the wild fury that in its scathing of the civilized world was shattering their most cherished illusions, they sought in vain for an explanation, and—without putting the fact into words—lit the lamp earlier than usual and took care to bolt the door. Usually it was fastened only on the latch, so that Madame could let herself in with the early morning; but to-night the darkness was unfriendly and the lonely valley held they knew not what of threatening.

Griselda, uneasily pondering on other matters, had no mind to give to the experiment of an omelette, and their supper was plain boiled eggs—boiled hard while she sat with wrinkled brow, unheeding of the flight of minutes. While they supped, their ears were always on the alert for a footstep or a hail from without; and perhaps for that reason they noticed as they had never noticed before the faint ghostly noises of the country—the night-calling bird and the shiver of leaves when the air stirred and sighed. They talked with effort and frequent pause, and with now and again a glance thrown sideways at the open window and the forest blackness behind it; there were no blinds to the windows, and but for the still, heavy heat they would have fastened the shutters and barred out the forest blackness. Perhaps they would have borne with the heat of a closed room had not both been ashamed to confess their fear of the window. In both their minds was the sense of being very far removed from humanity, the knowledge that between them and humanity was a lonely path and a house with its doors set open—a house deserted and half dismantled with a nameless grave before it. Unimaginative as they both were, they pictured the grave in the darkness with its roughly tied cross and its handful of wilting rosebuds.

They went upstairs earlier than usual, chiefly because they felt more comfortable when the windows below were fastened. William, coming last with the candle, took the added precaution of turning the key in the door at the foot of the stairs; and Griselda, though she made no remark, heard the click of the lock with a secret throb of relief. Upstairs they began by a little pretence of undressing—and then Griselda, with her hair down her back, sat close to William, with his coat off, and they held hands and talked in undertones in the intervals of listening for a footstep. The footstep never came; but it was not until close upon midnight that—knowing the early habits of the former tenants of the farm—they gave up all hope of hearing it and began to discuss their plans for the following day, on the presumption that they must leave the cottage and remove their luggage alone. Such unaided removal meant an earlier uprising than they had counted on—since if Madame did not prepare their breakfast they needs must prepare it themselves; and this misfortune realized, they decided to sit up no longer. They went to bed, but left the candle burning—as they said to each other, lest one of the Peys family should knock them up during the night. Neither slept much, partly from nervous uneasiness and partly from fear of oversleeping; but if they had guessed what a day would bring forth, neither would have slept at all.

CHAPTER VI

They had left their bedroom windows uncurtained, that the morning light might waken them, and they were hardly later than the August sun in opening their eyes on the world. Though they had slept but little, and by snatches, they turned out of bed without regret; the flood of sunlight brought warmth into their hearts and the shadowy horror of the night before was lifted with the mists of the valley; but all the same the place, once only faintly mysterious, was now actively malicious and distasteful, was tainted with a lurking dread. Thus to their pleasure at the thought of noise and London was added relief at the prospect of escape from a solitude grown fearful since yesterday. They dressed with haste and rising spirits; and it was with undisguised joy that they collected their few possessions and stuffed them into their hold-alls.

William, whose toilet and preparations for the journey were completed in advance of his wife's, descended first to the kitchen, where, in the continued and regretted absence of their housekeeper, he struggled valiantly with the making of breakfast while Griselda finished her packing. The meal so prepared fell short of complete success; coffee as brewed by William was not the same beverage as coffee prepared by Madame Peys, nor were its tepid attractions enhanced by the absence of their usual and plentiful ration of milk. Thanks to the defection of the Peys family, they were not only milkless but eggless; and such remains of bread and butter as they could find in the cupboard were the only accompaniment to William's suggestion of coffee. In the circumstances there was but little temptation to risk the loss of the Brussels train by lingering over the table and less than five minutes sufficed for their simple meal. Having despatched it, they strapped their hold-alls and stepped out briskly on their way to the station and home—the sun still low on the eastward ridge of the valley and the dew still heavy on the grass. They hardly turned to look back at the cottage, so glad were they to leave it behind them; and in the elation of their spirits they sped down the path with a quite unnecessary haste. They were escaping from nature and solitude, and their hearts sang cheerily of Bloomsbury.

When they rounded the bend in the path that brought them within sight of the farm their first thought was that the missing family had returned; for outside the gate were three horses, standing riderless and with heads near together. There was something reassuring in the sight of the beasts as they stood in the sunlight shifting and flicking their tails, something that gave the lie to the terrors of the night before; the presence of horses betokened the presence of men, and the presence of men dissipated the sense of mystery that had brooded over an empty house with a nameless grave in its garden. Griselda drew a comfortable breath of relief as she supposed they had time to call in and settle the last week's bill with Madame Peys.

"I do wish," she pondered regretfully, "that I could understand what she says. I must say I should like to know what the explanation is—about that grave ... I suppose they've come back to fetch away the rest of the furniture, and things—those aren't their horses, though!"

"No," William assented, considering the sleek strong beasts, "they have only got cart-horses ... I wonder." ...

A man stepped suddenly out from behind the shifting horses—so suddenly that they both started. He had been standing by the gate with the bridles gathered in his hand, hidden by his charges from William and Griselda as they had been hidden from him. When, hearing their voices, he stepped into sight, he stood with his heels together, very erect and staring at them—a young man squarely and sturdily built, with under his helmet a reddish face and a budding black moustache. He was clad in a tight-fitting greyish uniform, and a sword hung by his side. He stared and the pair stared back at him—curiously but not quite so openly.

"It's a soldier," Griselda commented—adding, like William, "I wonder——" They both wondered so much that they hesitated and slackened their pace; the presence of a military man but complicated the problem of the farm. Coupled with the absence of the Peys family, it revived their suspicions of the night before, their suspicions of crime and a hasty flight from justice ... and involuntarily their eyes turned to the garden, and sought the outline of the grave beyond the gooseberry bushes.

"It really does look," Griselda whispered, "as if there was something— not right."

As she whispered the soldier rapped out a loud monosyllable; it was enunciated so curtly and sharply that they started for the second time and came to an involuntary halt. For the space of a second or two they stood open-mouthed and flustered—and then Griselda, recovering from the shock, expressed her indignant opinion.

"How rude!" she said. "What does he shout at us like that for?"

"I suppose," her husband conjectured, "he wants us to stop."

"Well," said Griselda, "we have stopped." Her tone was nettled and embittered. It annoyed her to realize that, involuntarily and instinctively, she had obeyed an official order; it was not, she felt what her Leaders would expect from a woman of her training and calibre. It was that and not fear that disconcerted her—for, after the first shock of surprise at the man's rough manner, neither she nor her husband were in the least overawed; on the contrary, as they stood side by side with their baggage in their hands, gazing into the sunburnt face of the soldier, something of the contempt they felt for his species was reflected in their light-blue eyes. Of the two pairs of light-blue eyes William's perhaps were the more contemptuous: his anti-militarism was more habitual and ingrained than Griselda's.

What William looked at was a creature (the soldier) of whom he knew little and talked much; his experience of the man of war was purely insular, and his attitude towards him would have been impossible in any but a native of Britain. He came of a class—the English lower middle—which the rules of caste and tradition of centuries debarred from the bearing of arms; a class which might, in this connection, have adapted to its own needs the motto of the House of Rohan. "Roi ne puis; prince ne daigne; Rohan je suis," might have been suitably englished in the mouths of William's fellows as, "Officer I cannot be; private I will not be; tradesman or clerk I am." Further, he had lived in surroundings where the soldier was robbed of his terrors; to him the wearer of the king's uniform was not only a person to whom you alluded at Labour meetings with the certainty of raising a jeer, but a target at whom strikers threw brickbats and bottles with energy and practical impunity. Should the target grow restive under these attentions and proceed to return them in kind, it was denounced in Parliament, foamed at by the Press, and possibly court-martialled as a sop to indignant Labour. Thus handicapped it could hardly be looked on as a formidable adversary ... and William, without a thought of fear, stared the field-grey horseman in the eyes.

The field-grey horseman, on his side, stared the pair of civilians up and down—with a glance that matched the courtesy of his recent manner of address—until, having surveyed them sufficiently, he called over his shoulder to some one unseen within the house. There was something in his face and the tone of his loud-voiced hail that made the temper of Griselda stir within her; and for the second time that morning she wished for a command of the language of the country—this time for the purposes of sharp and scathing rebuke. As a substitute she assumed the air of cold dignity with which she had entered the taxi on the night of her protest at the meeting.

"Come on, William," she said. "Don't take any notice of him, dear."

The advice, though well meant, was unfortunate. As William attempted to follow both it and his wife, the soldier moved forward and struck him a cuff on the side of the head that deposited him neatly on the grass. Griselda, who—in order to convey her contempt for official authority and disgust at official insolence—had been pointedly surveying the meeting of hill and horizon, heard a whack and scuffle, a guttural grunt and a gasp; and turned to see William, with a hand to his cheek, lying prone at the feet of his assailant. She rounded on the man like a lion, and perhaps, with her suffragette training behind her, would have landed him a cuff in his turn; but as she raised her arm it was caught from behind and she found herself suddenly helpless in the grasp of a second grey-clad soldier—who, when he heard his comrade's hail, had come running out of the house.

"Let me go," she cried, wriggling in his grasp as she had wriggled aforetime in the hands of a London policeman, and kicking him deftly on the shins as she had been wont to kick Robert on his. For answer he shook her to the accompaniment of what sounded like curses—shook her vehemently, till her hat came off and her hair fell down, till her teeth rattled and the landscape danced about her. When he released her, with the final indignity of a butt with the knee in the rear, she collapsed on the grass by her husband's side in a crumpled, disreputable heap. There for a minute or two she lay gasping and inarticulate—until, as her breath came back and the landscape ceased to gyrate, she dragged herself up into a sitting position and thrust back the hair from her eyes. William, a yard or two away, was also in a sitting position with his hand pressed against his cheekbone; while over him stood the assailants in field-grey, apparently snapping out questions.

"I don't understand," she heard him protest feebly, "I tell you I don't understand. Griselda, can't you explain to them that I don't speak French?"

"Comprends pas," said Griselda, swallowing back tears of rage. "Comprends pas—so it's not a bit of good your talking to us. Parlez pas français—but that won't prevent me from reporting you for this disgraceful assault. You cowards—you abominable cowards! You're worse than the police at home, which is saying a good deal. I wonder you're not ashamed of yourselves. I've been arrested three times and I've never been treated like this."

At this juncture one of the men in field-grey seized William by the collar and proceeded to turn out his pockets—extracting from their recesses a purse, a pipe, a handkerchief, a fountain pen, and a green-covered Cook's ticket. He snapped back the elastic on the Cook's ticket, and turned the leaves that remained for the journey home.

"London," he ejaculated suddenly, pronouncing the vowels in un-English fashion as O's.

"London!" his companion echoed him—and then, as if moved by a common impulse, they called on the name of Heinz.

There was an answering hail from the farmhouse kitchen, whence issued promptly a fattish young man with a mug in his hand, and a helmet tilted on his nose. With him the assailants of William and Griselda entered into rapid and throaty explanations; whereat Heinz nodded assentingly as he advanced down the garden path to the gate, surveying the captives with interest and a pair of little pigs'-eyes. Having reached the gate he leaned over it, mug in hand, and looked down at William and Griselda.

"English," he said in a voice that was thicker than it should have been at so early an hour of the morning; "English—you come from London? ... I have been two years in London; that is why I speak English. I was with a hairdresser in the Harrow Road two years; and I know also the Strand and the Angel and Buckingham Palace and the Elephant." (He was plainly proud of his acquaintance with London topography.) "All of them I know, and when we arrive in London I shall show them all to my friends." He waved his hand vaguely and amiably to indicate his grey-clad companions. "You come from London, but you shall not go back there, because you are now our prisoners. I drink your damn bad health and the damn bad health of your country and the damn bad health of your king."

He suited the action to the word and drained his mug; and having drained it till it stood upright upon his nose, proceeded to throw it over his shoulder to shatter on the brick path. Whether from natural good temper or the cheering effect of potations his face was wreathed in an amiable smile as he crossed his arms on the bar of the gate and continued to address his audience—

"We shall take you to our officer and you will be prisoners, and if you are spies you will be shot."

There was something so impossible about the announcement that William and Griselda felt their courage return with a rush. Moreover, though the words of Heinz were threatening the aspect of Heinz was not; his fat young face with its expansive and slightly inebriated smile was ridiculous rather than terrifying, even under the brim of a helmet. William, thankful for the English acquired during the two years' hairdressing in the Harrow Road, admonished him with a firmness intended to sober and dismay.

"This is not a time for silly jokes. I am afraid that you do not realize the seriousness of the situation. I shall feel it my duty to make a full report to your superiors—when you will find it is no laughing matter. My wife and I, proceeding quietly to the station, have been grossly and violently assaulted by your two companions. We gave them no provocation, and the attack was entirely uncalled for. I repeat, I shall feel it my duty to report their conduct in the very strongest terms."

He felt as he spoke that the reproof would have carried more weight had it been delivered in a standing position; but his head still reeled from the stinging cuff it had received and he felt safer where he was—on the ground. It annoyed him that the only apparent effect of his words upon Heinz was a widening of his already wide and owlish smile.

"Oh, you'll report their conduct, will you?" he repeated pleasantly and thickly. "And who will you report it to, old son?"

William stiffened at the familiarity, and the tone of his reply was even colder and more dignified than that of the original rebuke.

"To the nearest police authority; I shall not leave Belgium until my complaint has been attended to. If necessary I shall apply for redress to the British Consul in Brussels."

The expansive smile on the face of Heinz was suddenly ousted by an expression of infinite astonishment. His fat chin dropped, his little eyes widened, and he pushed back his helmet, that he might stare the better at William.

"Say it again," he demanded—slowly and as if doubtful of his ears, "You shall apply to the British Consul—the British Consul at Brussels?"

"Certainly," William assured him firmly; and Griselda echoed "Certainly." The threat they judged had made the desired impression, for so blank and disturbed was the countenance of Heinz that his two companions broke into guttural questioning. The former hairdresser checked them with a gesture and addressed himself once more to William.

"I think," he announced, "you are balmy on the crumpet, both of you. Balmy," he repeated, staring from one to the other and apparently sobered by the shock of his own astonishment. Suddenly a gleam of intelligence lit up his little pig's-eyes—he leaned yet further over the gate, pointed a finger and queried—

"You do not read the newspapers?"

"As a rule I do," William informed him, "but we have not seen any lately—not since we left England."

"And how long is it since you left England?"

William told him it was over three weeks.

"Three weeks," the other repeated, "three weeks without newspapers ... and I think you do not speak French, eh?"

"My wife," William answered, "understands it—a little. But we neither of us speak it." His manner was pardonably irritated, and if he had not judged it imprudent he would have refused point-blank to answer this purposeless catechism. Nor was his pardonable irritation lessened when amusement once more gained the upper hand in Heinz. Suddenly and unaccountably he burst into hearty laughter—rocked and trembled with it, holding to the gate and wiping the tears from his cheeks. Whatever the joke it appealed also to his comrades, who, once it was imparted between Heinz's paroxysms, joined their exquisite mirth to his own. The three stood swaying in noisy merriment, while Griselda, whitefaced and tight-lipped, and William with a fast disappearing left eye awaited in acute and indignant discomfort some explanation of a jest that struck them as untimely. It came only when Heinz had laughed himself out. Wiping the tears once more from his eyes, and with a voice still weakened by pleasurable emotion, he gave them in simple and unpolished language the news of the European cataclysm.

"I tell you something, you damn little ignorant silly fools. There is a war since you came to Belgium."

Probably they thought it was a drunken jest, for they made no answer beyond a stare, and Heinz proceeded with enjoyment.

"A War. The Greatest that ever was. Germany and Austria—and Russia and France and Belgium and England and Servia."

He spoke slowly, dropping out his words that none might fail of their effect and ticked off on a finger the name of each belligerent.

"Our brave German troops have conquered Belgium and that is why we are here. We shall also take Paris and we shall also take Petersburg and we shall also take London. We shall march through Regent Street and Leicester Square and over Waterloo Bridge. Our Kaiser Wilhelm shall make peace in Westminster Abbey, and we shall take away all your colonies. What do you think of that, you damn little fools?"

There are statements too large as there are statements too wild for any but the unusually imaginative to grasp at a first hearing. Neither William nor Griselda had ever entertained the idea of a European War; it was not entertained by any of their friends or their pamphlets. Rumours of war they had always regarded as foolish and malicious inventions set afloat in the interest of Capitalism and Conservatism with the object of diverting attention from Social Reform or the settlement of the Woman Question; and to their ears, still filled with the hum of other days, the announcement of Heinz was even such a foolish invention. Nor, even had they given him credence, would they in these first inexperienced moments have been greatly perturbed or alarmed; their historical ignorance was so profound, they had talked so long and so often in terms of war, that they had come to look on the strife of nations as a glorified scuffle on the lines of a Pankhurst demonstration. Thus Griselda, taught by *The Suffragette*, used the one word "battle" for a small street row and the fire and slaughter of Eylau—or would have so used it, had she known of the slaughter of Eylau. And that being the case, Heinz's revelation of ruin and thunder left her calm—disappointingly so.

"I think," she said loftily, in answer to his question, "that you are talking absolute nonsense."

There are few men who like to be balked of a sensation and Heinz was not among them. He reddened with annoyance at the lack of success of his bombshell.

"You do not believe it," he said. "You do not believe that our brave German troops have taken Belgium and will shortly take Paris and London? Very well, I will teach you. I will show you. You shall come with us to our officer and you shall be shot for spies."

He came through the gate and clambered into his saddle, his companions following suit; William and Griselda instinctively scrambled to their feet and stood gazing up in uncertainty at the three grey mounted men.

"Get on," said Heinz with a jerk of his head down the valley; and as William and Griselda still stood and gazed his hand went clap to his side and a sword flashed out of its sheath. Griselda shrieked in terror as it flashed over William's head—and William bawled and writhed with pain as it came down flat on his shoulder.

"Get on," Heinz repeated—adding, "damn you!" and worse—as the blade went up again; and William and Griselda obeyed him without further hesitation. Their heads were whirling and their hearts throbbing with rage; but they choked back its verbal expression and stumbled down the valley path—in the clutch of brute force and with their world crumbling about them. It was a most unpleasant walk—or rather trot; they were bruised, they were aching from the handling they had received, and their breath came in sobs from the pace they were forced to keep up. Did they slacken it even for an instant and fall level with the walking horses, Heinz shouted an order to "Hurry, you swine!" and flashed up his threatening sword; whereupon, to keep out of its painful and possibly dangerous reach, they forced themselves to a further effort and broke into a shambling canter. The sweat poured off them as they shambled and gasped, casting anxious glances at the horses' heads behind them; and their visible distress, their panting and their impotent anger, was a source of obvious and unrestrained gratification to Heinz and his jovial companions. They jeered at the captives' clumsy running and urged them to gallop faster. When Griselda tripped over a tussock and sprawled her length on the grass, they applauded her downfall long and joyously and begged her to repeat the performance. The jeers hurt more than the shaking, and she staggered to her feet with tears of wretchedness and outraged dignity running openly down her nose—seeking in vain for that sense of moral superiority and satisfaction in martyrdom which had always sustained her en route to the cells of Bow Street. She hated the three men who jeered at her miseries and could have killed them with pleasure; every fibre of her body was quivering with wrath and amazement. Neither she nor William could speak—they had no breath left in them to speak; but every now and then as they shambled along they turned their hot faces to look at each other—and saw, each, a beloved countenance red with exertion and damp with perspiration, a pair of bewildered blue eyes and a gasping open mouth.... So they trotted down the valley, humiliated, dishevelled, indignant, but still incredulous—while their world crumbled about them and Europe thundered and bled.

CHAPTER VII

Tuchman - Guns of August

Looking back on the morning in the month of August, nineteen hundred and fourteen, when he made his first acquaintance with war as the soldier understands it, William Tully realized that fear, real fear, was absent from his heart until he witnessed the shooting of the hostages. Until that moment he had been unconvinced, and, because unconvinced, unafraid; he had been indignant, flustered, physically sore and inconvenienced; but always at the back of his mind was the stubborn belief that the pains and indignities endured by himself and his wife would be dearly paid for by the perpetrators. He could conceive as yet of no state of society in which Law and the bodily immunity of the peaceful citizen was not the ultimate principle; and even the sight of a long grey battalion of infantry plodding dustily westward on the road by the river had not convinced him of war and the meaning of war. They came on the trudging torrent of men as they debouched from the valley on to the main road; and their captors halted them on the grass at the roadside until the close grey ranks had passed. William and Griselda were thankful for the few minutes' respite and breathing-space; they wiped their hot faces and Griselda made ineffectual attempts to tidy her tumbled hair. She was reminded by her pressing need of hairpins that they had left their bags on the scene of their misfortune, outside the farmhouse gate; they conversed about the loss in undertones, and wondered if the bags would be recovered. They were not without hopes, taking into account the loneliness of the neighbourhood.... When the battalion, with its tail of attendant grey carts, had passed, Heinz ordered them forward again—and they moved on, fifty yards or so behind the last of the grey carts, and trusting that their goal was at hand.

"If they're only taking us as far as the village," Griselda panted hopefully.

They were—to the familiar little village with its miniature railway station between the river and the cliff. The column of infantry plodded dustily through and past it, but Heinz followed the rear-guard only halfway down the street before he shouted to his prisoners to halt. They halted—with an alacrity born of relief and a sense of the wisdom of prompt obedience to orders—before an unpretentious white building with a sentry stationed on either side of the door. Heinz swung himself down from his horse and went into the house, leaving William and Griselda in charge of his comrades and standing at the side of the road.

William and Griselda looked about them. They had passed through the place several times and were accustomed enough to its usual appearance to be aware of the change that had come over it. The rumbling grey carts behind which they had tramped were already at the end of the village; they could see all the sunlit length of the street and take stock of the new unfamiliar life which filled it from end to end.

It was a life masculine and military; an odd mixture of iron order and disorder; of soldiers on duty and soldiers taking their ease. The street itself was untidy and littered as they had never seen it before; its centre had been swept clear, so that traffic might pass unhindered, but the sides of the road were strewn with a jetsam of fragmentary lumber. A country cart that had lost a wheel sat clumsily in front of the church near a jumble of broken pottery, and a chair with its legs in the air was neighboured by trusses of straw. All down the street the doors stood widely open—here and there a house with starred or shattered windows looked unkempt and forlornly shabby. Beyond shivered panes and occasional litter of damaged crockery and furniture there was no sign of actual violence; the encounter that had taken place there—a cavalry skirmish between retreating Belgian and advancing German—had left few traces behind it.

The civilians of the village, with hardly an exception, were invisible. The landlord of the café was serving his soldier customers, and two labourers were unloading sacks, from a miller's dray under the eye of a guard; and when William and Griselda had been waiting for a few minutes an old man crossed the road hurriedly from opposite house to house—emerging from shelter like a rabbit from its burrow and vanishing with a swift running hobble. As for women, they saw only two—whom they were not to forget easily.

They stood, the two women, a few yards away on the further side of the road; almost opposite the door by which Heinz had disappeared and with their eyes continually fixed on it. One—the elder—was stout and grey-headed, very neatly dressed in black with a black woollen scarf on her shoulders; her hands were folded, meeting on her breast, and every now and then she bent her head over them while her lips moved slowly and soundlessly. At such moments she closed her eyes, but when she lifted her head again they turned steadily to the door. The woman who stood beside her was taller and younger, middle-aged, upright, and angular; she also wore a black dress, and above her sharp and yellowish features an unbecoming black hat—a high-crowned hat with upstanding and rusty black bows. What struck you about her at the first glance was her extreme respectability—in the line of her lean shoulders, in the dowdily conventional hat; at a second, the fact that her mouth was a line, so tightly were her lips compressed. She also stood with her eyes fixed on the door. William and Griselda looked at the pair curiously; it was odd and uncomfortable to see them standing at the side of the road, their clothes dusted by passing cars, not moving or speaking to each other.

For the rest, from end to end of the street there were only soldiers in sight. Soldiers taking their noisy ease at the tables outside the café—any number of them crowded round the little green tables while the sweating landlord ran to and fro with a jug or a tray of glasses and an obvious desire to propitiate. Other soldiers, less noisy, led a string of horses to water; and a rigid file of them with rifles grounded, was drawn up on the further side of the street not far from the waiting women; some ten or a dozen of motionless helmeted automata, with a young officer, a ruddy-faced boy, pacing up and down the road in front of them. Through a gap in the row of white houses William and Griselda saw another group of men in their shirt-sleeves at work on the railway line—the line that should have taken them to Brussels; they seemed to be repairing some damage to the permanent way; and further down the village two or three soldier mechanics were busied inquisitively at the bonnet of a heavy grey car drawn up at the side of the road. While they waited and watched other heavy grey cars of the same pattern rumbled into the street and along it; and motor cycles one after another hooted and clanked past them to vanish in a smothering trail of dust.

In after days William tried vainly to recall what he felt and thought in the long hot minutes while they waited for Heinz to reappear and for something to happen. He supposed that it was the fiercer sensations of the time that followed which deadened the impressions of the half-hour or so during which they stood in the sunny street expecting they knew not what; and though he remembered, and remembered vividly, the outward show and manner of the place—its dusty road, its swarming soldiers, its passing cars and cycles and the bearing of the two silent women—the memory brought with it no hint of his accompanying attitude of mind. All he knew was that he had not been seriously alarmed.... He might have recalled his impressions with more success had he and Griselda discussed at the time their new and surprising experiences; but an attempt to enter into conversation was promptly checked by one of their attendant guards. What he actually said was unintelligible, but his manner conveyed his meaning and thereafter the captives considered their situation in silence.

He did not know how long it was before the hostages came out into the street; but he remembered—it was his first distinct memory of a vivid personal impression—the instantaneous thrill of relief and excitement with which, after their dreary wait, he saw the first signs of movement at the sentry-guarded door. A man—a soldier—came out swiftly and went to the boy-officer, who thereupon stopped his pacing; there was a clicking of heels, a salute and a message rapidly delivered; the boy-officer turned and shouted to his men and, his men moved at the word, their rifles going to their shoulders, as if by the impulse of one will. William's eye was caught and held by the oiled swiftness, the mechanical simultaneousness of the movement; he stared at the line of uniforms, now rigidly inactive again, till a hand from behind gripped his collar and impelled him urgently sideways. One of his captors had adopted this simple method of informing him that way must be made for those about to issue from the door of the sentry-guarded house. He choked angrily and brought up against the wall—to which Griselda, taking warning, had hastily backed herself. He was still gasping when the little procession came out; a soldier leading it, a couple more with bayonets fixed—two civilians walking together—a couple more soldiers with bayonets fixed and last of all an officer, a fattish, youngish, moustachioed man whom the sentries stiffened to salute. He came a little behind his men, paused on the step and stood there framed in the doorway with his hand resting on his sword, the embodiment of conscious authority; the others, the two civilians and their guard, went on to the middle of the road. There, in the middle of the road, they also halted—the soldiers smartly, the captives uncertainly—and William saw the two civilians clearly.

One was a short and rotund little man who might have been sixty to sixty-five and might have been a local tradesman—nearly bald and with drooping moustaches, rather like a stout little seal. Essentially an ordinary and unpretentious creature, he was obviously aiming at dignity; his chin was lifted at an angle that revealed the measure of the roll of fat that rested on his collar, and he walked almost with a strut, as if he were attempting to march. Afterwards William remembered that he had seen on the little man's portly stomach some sort of insignia or ribbon; at the time it conveyed nothing to him, but he was told later that it was the outward token of a mayor. He remembered also that the little man's face was pale, with a sickly yellow-grey pallor; and that as he came down the steps with his head held up the drooping moustache quivered and the fat chin beneath it twitched spasmodically. There was something extraordinarily pitiful about his attempt at a personal dignity which nature had wholly denied him; William felt the appeal in it even before he grasped the situation the meaning and need of the pose.

The man who walked on his left hand was taller and some years younger—middle-aged, slightly stooping and with slightly grizzled hair and beard. He belonged to an ordinary sedentary type, and William, thinking him over later, was inclined to set him down a schoolmaster, or perhaps a clerk. He wore steel-rimmed eye-glasses and his black coat was shiny on the back and at the elbows; he had none of his fellow's pomposity, and walked dragging his feet and with his eyes bent on the ground. He raised them only when, as they halted in the middle of the road, the respectable woman in black called out something—one word, perhaps his name—came up to him and caught him by the shoulder. He answered her quickly and very briefly—with hardly more than a word—and for a second or two after he had spoken she stood quite still, with her hand resting on his shoulder. Then, suddenly, her sallow face contorted, her thin mouth writhed and from it there came a cry that was too fierce to be called a groan and too hoarse to be called a scream; she flung herself forward on the neck of the grizzled man and her lean black arms went round it. He tried to speak to her again, but she silenced him by drawing down his head to her breast; she held it to her breast and pressed it there; she rocked and swayed a little from side to side, fondling the grizzled hair and kissing it to a stream of broken endearment. Her grief was animal, alike in its unrestraint and its terrible power of expression; convention fell away from her; in her tidy dress and with her dowdy hat slipping to one shoulder she was primitive woman crooning over her dying mate.... When she was seized and drawn away from her man, her curved fingers clung to his garments. Two soldiers held her and she writhed between them choking out a hoarse incoherent appeal to the officer standing in the frame of the doorway with his hand on the hilt of his sword; she went on crying herself hoarser as her captors urged her further down the street and at last, in mercy to those who looked on, out of sight through an open doorway. William had his hands to his ears when the door shut. No one, in spite of the persistence of her cries, came out into the street to inquire the cause of her grief; but it seemed to William afterwards that he had been aware here and there of furtive faces that appeared at upper windows.

While they forced the dowdy woman away from him her man stood motionless, turned away from her with his head bent and his eyes on the ground, so that he started when a soldier came up behind him and tapped him sharply on the arm. The soldier—he had stripes on his sleeve and seemed a person of authority—held a handkerchief dangling from his hand; and, seeing it, the grizzled-haired captive removed his steel-rimmed eyeglasses.

"Don't look," said William under his breath. "Griselda, don't look."

For the first time mortal fear had seized him by the throat and shaken him. He knew now that he stood before death itself, and the power to inflict death, and his heart was as water within him. His wife was beside him—and when he realized (as he did later on with shame) that the spasm of terror in those first moments of comprehension had been stronger than the spasm of pity, he excused it by the fact of her presence. His fear in its forecast of evil took tangible shape. Griselda at his elbow had her eyes and her mouth wide open; she was engrossed, fascinated—and he was afraid, most horribly afraid, that in her amazement, her righteous pity, she might say or do something that would bring down wrath upon them. He remembered how bold she had been in the face of a crowd, how uplifted by sacred enthusiasm! ... He plucked her by the sleeve when he whispered to her not to look—but she went on staring, wide-eyed and wide-mouthed, for the first time unresponsive to his touch and the sound of his voice.

They bandaged the eyes of the two prisoners—the rotund pompous little mayor and the man who might have been a schoolmaster. All his life William remembered the look of the rotund mayor with a bandage covering him from forehead to nose-tip and his grey moustache quivering beneath it—a man most pitifully afraid to die, yet striving to die as the situation demanded. And he remembered how, at the moment the bandage was knotted on the mayor's head, there stepped up to him quietly the stout old woman who had stood praying on the further side of the road with her eyes fixed upon the door. She held up a little crucifix and pressed it to the quivering grey moustache.... Griselda clutched William by the wrist and he thought she was going to cry out.

"Don't, darling, don't!" he whispered. "Oh, darling, for both our sakes!" ...

He did not know whether it was his appeal or her own terror and amazement that restrained her from speech—but she stood in silence with her fingers tightened on his wrist. He wished she would look away, he wished he could look away himself; he tried for an instant to close his eyes, but the not-seeing was worse than sight, and he had to open them again. As he opened them a car roared by raising a smother of dust; but as the cloud of its passage settled he saw that the two blindfolded men were standing with their backs to a blank wall—a yellow-washed, eight-foot garden wall with the boughs of a pear-tree drooping over it. It was opposite the yellow-washed wall, across the road, that the file of soldiers was drawn up; the captives were facing the muzzles of their rifles and the red-faced boy-officer had stationed himself stiffly at the farther end of the file. The dust settled and died down—and there followed (so it seemed to William) an agony of waiting for something that would not happen. Long beating seconds (three or four of them at most) while two men stood upright with bandaged eyes and rifles pointed at their hearts; long beating seconds, while a bird fluted in the pear-tree—a whistle-note infinitely careless.... And then (thank God for it!) a voice and a report that were as one.... The man with the grizzled hair threw out an arm and toppled with his face in the dust; the mayor slid sideways against the wall with the blood dribbling from his mouth.

CHAPTER VIII

Fundamentally William was no more of a coward than the majority of his fellow-men, and, put to it, he would have emulated the shivering little mayor and tried to strut gamely to his end; it was as much sheer bewildered amazement as the baseness of bodily terror that had him by the throat when he saw the hostages done to death—sickening and shaking him and, for the moment, depriving him of self-control. Never before, in all his twenty-eight years, had he seen a man come to his end; so far death had touched him only once, and but slightly, by the unseen passing of a mother he had not loved; thus the spectacle of violent and bloody dying would of itself have sufficed to unnerve and unman him. To the natural shrinking from that spectacle, to his natural horror at the slaying of helpless men, to his pity and physical nausea was added the impotent, gasping confusion of the man whose faith has been uprooted, who is face to face with the incredible. Before his eyes had been enacted the impossible—the ugly and brutal impossible—and beneath his feet the foundations of the earth were reeling. The iron-mouthed guns and the marching columns which had hitherto passed him as a dusty pageant took life and meaning in his eyes; they were instruments of the ugly impossible. There was meaning too in the lonely grave and in the lonely house—whence men had fled in terror of such scenes as his eyes had witnessed. So far, to him, the limit of human savagery had been the feeding through the nose of divers young women who, infected with the virus of martyrdom, demanded to be left to die—and now he had witnessed the killing of men who desired most greatly to live. At the time he did not—because he could not—analyse either the elements of the situation or his own attitude towards it; but he knew afterwards, vaguely but surely, that in that one bewildering and ruthless moment the heart of his faith was uprooted—his faith in that large vague entity the People, in the power of Public Opinion and Talk, in the power of the Good Intention.... Until that moment he had confounded the blunder with the crime, the mistaken with the evilly intentioned. It had not seemed to him possible that a man could disagree with him honestly and out of the core of his heart; it had not seemed to him possible that the righteous could be righteous and yet err. He knew now, as by lightning flash, that he, Faraday, a thousand others, throwing scorn from a thousand platforms on the idea of a European War, had been madly, wildly, ridiculously wrong—and the knowledge stunned and blinded him. They had meant so well, they had meant so exceedingly well—and yet they had prophesied falsely and fact had given them the lie. Until that moment he had been in what he called politics the counterpart of the Christian Scientist, despising and denying the evil that now laughed triumphant in his face. With its triumph perforce he was converted. War was: men were shot against walls. Converted, though as yet he knew not to what form of unknown faith.

He did not see what became of the two dead bodies—whither they were taken or by whom they were buried—for they had barely fallen to the ground and his eyes were still closed that he might not look on the blood that was dribbling from the mayor's moustache when a hand tapped him smartly on the shoulder and he found Heinz standing beside him. He had a glimpse of men moving round the bodies, a glimpse of his wife's face staring and sickly, another of a passing motor-cycle, and then Heinz turned him to the door where the sentries stood on guard. With his captor's hand on his shoulder he went into the low white house, along a little passage on the ground floor and into a room on the right, at the back of the house; Griselda coming after him, still staring and white-faced and likewise with a hand on her shoulder. In the room—large and sunny with windows looking on to a garden—was a man in uniform and spectacles writing at a table, and, erect and complacent beside him, the fattish moustachioed officer who had watched the execution from the doorstep. He was lighting a cigar with a hand that did not tremble. William and Griselda were escorted by their guards into the middle of the room and planted there, standing in front of him.

After what he had seen, and with the memory of Heinz's threats, William Tully believed most firmly that he too was about to die; and with the conviction there filled his heart (as it would have filled the heart of any honest lover) a great and intolerable pity for Griselda, his new-made wife. She, the woman, would be left where he, the man, would be taken—and he dared not turn his head towards her lest he might see her face instinct with the agony of the coming parting, lest, foreseeing and resisting it, she should fling her arms about him and croon over him as the sallow-faced woman in respectable black had crooned over the head of her man. Her meanings, the meanings of a woman unknown, had torn at his inmost heart; how should he bear it when Griselda, his darling, clung fast to him and cried in vain for pity? ... That he might not see Griselda's face even with the tail of an eye he stared hard and steadily over the officer's shoulder. He never forgot the wall-paper beyond the well-filled grey uniform; it was dingy mud and orange as to ground with a ponderous pattern of clumped and climbing vegetables. In one spot, opposite the window, where a blaze of sunlight struck it, the mud and orange was transfigured to shining gold—and William knew suddenly that he had never seen sunlight before. For the first time he saw it as vivid glory from heaven—when his eyes (as he thought) would soon close on its splendour for ever. Not only his sight but his every sense was alert and most sharply intense; on a sudden the thudding of guns in the distance was threateningly nearer at hand, and, in the interval between the gun-bursts, a wasp beating up and down the window-pane filled the room with a spiteful humming.

It was while he stood waiting for the doom he believed to be certain, while the German captain looked him up and down and addressed curt unintelligible questions to those who had made him their prisoner—that there stirred in the breast of William Tully the first faint sense of nationality. He did not recognize it as such, and it was not to be expected that he should, since his life for the last few strenuous years had been largely moulded on the principle that the love of one's country was a vice to be combated and sneered at. If you had told him a short day earlier that the thought of the soil he was born on could move and thrill and uplift him, he would have stared and despised you as a jingo, that most foolish and degraded of survivals; yet with his eyes (as he thought) looking their last on the blazing gold that was sunlight, with the sword suspended over his trembling head, something that was not only his pitiful love for Griselda, something that was more than his decent self-respect, fluttered and stirred within him and called on him to play the man. It bade him straighten his back before men of an outlandish race, it bade him refrain from pleading and weakness before those who were not of his blood; and for the first time for many years he thought of himself as a national, a man of the English race. Not consciously as yet and with no definite sense of affection for England or impulse to stand by her and serve her; but with a vague, unreasoning, natural longing for home and the narrow things of home. It mattered not that the England he longed for was small, suburban, crowded and noisily pretentious; he craved for it in the face of death, as other men crave for their spacious fenlands or the sweep of their open downs. England as he knew her called him, not with the noisy call of yesterday, but in a voice less strident and more tender; he knew now that it was dreadful to die away from her. Instinctively, thinking on London, he drew himself up to the height of his five foot five and—as the mayor had done before him—he lifted his chin in would-be defiance and dignity.

There—with the attempt to subdue the trembling flesh and defy brute insolence and tyranny—the resemblance between the two men's cases ended. For the time being William ran no risk of a violent and bloody ending; there was no further need of an example and he had offended the conqueror only by his poor little presence. Further—though he expressed his enjoyment of it less noisily and emphatically than his three subordinates had done—the humour of his prisoner's situation appealed to Heinz's superior officer almost as much as it had appealed to Heinz himself. He grinned perceptibly as he questioned the couple in his somewhat halting English; chuckled audibly when they confirmed his subordinate's statement as to their complete ignorance of the European upheaval; and when he had elicited the fact that the hapless pair had been spending their honeymoon in the secluded valleys of Ardennes he removed his cigar from his moustachioed lips that he might chuckle long and unhindered.

"Honeymoon," he repeated, his stout shoulders trembling with merriment. "In a nice, quiet place, wiz no one to interrupt zee kissings. Never mind—you will have a very good honeymoon with us and you will very soon be able to go back to England. Just so soon as the Sherman Army shall have been there. You should be very pleased that you are safe with us: it is more dangerous to be in London."

William, with his nerves tuned up to face a firing party, withered miserably under heavy jocularity. He knew instinctively that his life was saved to him; but the assurance of safety was conveyed in a jeer, and at the moment (so oddly are we made) the jeer hurt more than the assurance of safety relieved him. He had mastered his anguish and strung himself up—to be treated as a figure of fun; the spectacled clerk at the writing-table was laughing so heartily that he had to remove his glasses and wipe them before he continued his labours. William tingled all over with helpless rage as Griselda tingled beside him. But yesterday he would have told you loftily that both he and his wife were inured to public, above all to official, ridicule; but it is one thing to brave ridicule with an approving audience in the background, another to face it unapplauded, uncrowned with the halo of the martyr.... They reddened and quivered whilst incomprehensible witticisms passed between the captain and his clerk. It was an intense relief when a nod and a brief order signified that the jest was sufficiently enjoyed and their audience with the captain at an end. They were too thankful even to resent the roughness with which Heinz collared his man while his comrade collared Griselda.

CHAPTER IX

One of the features of the interview that struck William later on was this—during all the long minutes that it lasted Griselda had spoken no words. For once the tumult and amazement of her soul was beyond her glib power of expression and it was only as they came into the open air that—for the first time since she had seen the hostages die—she unclosed her lips and spoke.

"What are they going to do with us?" she asked. Her voice was husky and uncertain, and the words came out in little jerks.

William gave the question no answer: for one thing because his ignorance of their destiny was as thorough as his wife's; for another because speech, by reason of Heinz's firm grip on his collar, was so difficult as to be almost impossible. The man had his knuckles thrust tightly between shirt and skin; William purpled and gasped as he trotted down the street with a collar stud pressing on his windpipe. Behind him when he started came Griselda and her guard; as he could not twist his head to look over his shoulder he had no suspicion that the couples had parted company, and it was not until his captor turned him sharply to the right down a by-road leading to the station that he discovered, in rounding the corner, that his wife and her escort were no longer following in his footsteps. The momentary sidelong glimpse he caught of the road gave him never a sight of Griselda; she had vanished without word or sign. For a moment he could hardly believe it and walked on stupidly in silence; then, the stupor passing, his terror found voice and he clamoured.

"Where's my wife?" he cried out and writhed instinctively to free himself. His reward was a tightening of the German's strangle-hold, some most hearty abuse and some even heartier kicks. Under the punishment he lost his foothold and would have fallen but for Heinz's clutch upon his collar; when the punishment was over he was brought up trembling and choking. In that moment he suffered the fiercest of torments, the fire of an ineffectual hate. He hated Heinz and could have torn him; but he had been taught the folly of blind wrestling with the stronger and, for Griselda's sake, he swallowed his fury and cringed.

"Where is she?" he begged most humbly and pitifully as Heinz thrust him forward again. "For mercy's sake tell me what you have done with my wife—with my wife? ... If you will only let me know where she is? That's all—just to let me know."

He was answered by the silence of contempt and a renewed urge along the road; he obeyed because he could do no other, whimpering aloud in the misery of this new and sharpest of misfortunes. As he pled and whimpered terrible thoughts came hurrying into his brain; all things were possible in these evil times and among these evil men—and there was a dreadful, hideously familiar phrase anent "licentious soldiery": a phrase that had once been just a phrase and that was now a present horror beating hard in his burning head. He stumbled on with the tears running down his cheeks, and discovered suddenly that he was whispering under his breath the name of God—all things else having failed him. He did not realize that he was sobbing and shedding great tears until halfway along the road when a German soldier met them. The man as he passed turned his head to laugh at the sight of a face grotesque and distorted in its wretchedness; whereupon there flared up again in William that new sense of blood and breed and with it an instant rush of shame that he had wept before these—Germans! He gulped back his tears, strove to stiffen his face and clenched his hands to endure.

He had need in the hours that came after of all his powers of endurance alike of body and of mind. The day that already seemed age-long was far from being at its height when Griselda was taken away from him and all through the heat till close upon sundown he was put to hard physical toil. Level with the village the railway line had been torn up and the little wayside station was a half-burnt mass of wreckage; a detachment of retreating Belgians had done their best to destroy it, had derailed an engine and half a dozen trucks and done such damage as time allowed to a stretch of the permanent way. In its turn a detachment of Germans was hard at work at removal of the wreckage and repairs to the line; and into their service they had pressed such villagers as had not fled at their approach. A cowed, unhappy band they toiled and sweated, dug, carried loads and levelled the broken soil; some stupidly submissive, some openly sullen to their captors, some pitiably eager to please: all serfs for the time being and all of them ignorant of what the next hour might bring forth of further terror or misfortune.

To this captive little company William Tully was joined, handed over by Heinz to its taskmaster—to become of them all the most pitiable, because for the first time in all his days set to bend his back and use his muscles in downright labour of the body. What to others was merely hardship, to him became torment unspeakable; he wearied, he sweated, he ached from head to heel. When he pulled at heavy wreckage he cut his soft clumsy fingers; when he dragged a load or carried it he strained his unaccustomed back. His hands bled and blistered and the drops of perspiration poured off him; when he worked slowly because of his weariness or lack of skill, authority made no allowance for either and a blow often followed a curse. Sometimes incomprehensible orders were shouted at him and he would run to obey confusedly, for fear of the punishment meted out without mercy to the dilatory—guessing at what was required of him, sometimes rightly and sometimes wrongly. The day remained on his mind as an impression of muddled terror and panic intense and unceasing.

When he thought he was not being watched he would lift his head from his toil and strain his eyes this way and that in the hope of a glimpse of Griselda. Unspeakably greater than his fear for himself was the measure of his fear for his wife. He knew that somewhere she must be held by force in the same way that he was held, otherwise she would have sought him out long ere this, and, even if not allowed to approach or speak would have managed to see him and make him some sign that his heart might be set at rest. His brain was giddy with undefined horror and once or twice he started and raised his head imagining that Griselda was calling to him. Once when he looked up his eye caught the bluff towering over the valley and he remembered with an incredulous shock that it was only yesterday that he and his wife, stretched out on the turf, had watched the galloping of the ants of soldiers beneath it—that it was not a day since they had listened indifferently to the mutter of guns in the distance and talked with superior detachment of manoeuvres and the folly of militarism. Side by side on the short-cropped turf they had watched unmoved and listened without misgiving. Only yesterday—nay, only this morning when the sun rose—the world was the world and not hell.

He knew though, engrossed by his private agony, he did not give it much heed, that all the afternoon there was heavy traffic on the road that ran through the village, traffic going this way and that; now and again through the clatter of the work around him its rumble came to his ears. Noisy cars went by and heavy guns, regiments of infantry and once or twice a company of swift-moving horse that sped westward in a flurry of dust. As the hot, industrious hours crawled by even his terror for Griselda was swallowed up in the numbing and all-pervading sense of bodily exhaustion and ill-being, in the consciousness of throbbing head, parched mouth and miserable back. At midday when the captives were doled out a ration of meat and bread he lay like a log for the little space during which he was allowed to rest; and, resting, he dreaded from the bottom of his soul the inevitable call back to work. With it all was the hopeless, the terrifying sense of isolation; he was removed even from his fellow-sufferers, held apart from them not only by the barrier of their alien speech but by his greater feebleness and greater physical suffering. Only once during those sun-smitten and aching hours did he feel himself akin to any of the men around him—when a flat-capped, sturdy young German soldier, taking pity on his manifest unfitness for the work, muttered some good-natured, incomprehensible encouragement and handed him a bottle to drink from. The sharp taste of beer was a liquid blessing to William's dry tongue and parched throat; he tilted the bottle and drank in great gulps till he choked; whereat the flat-capped German boy-soldier laughed consumedly but not unkindly.

It must have been well on in the afternoon—for the shadows were beginning to lengthen though the sun burned hotly as ever—when over the noises of the toil around him and over the rumble of traffic on the road the persistent beat of guns became loud enough to make itself noticeable. All day William had heard it at intervals; during his brief rest at midday it had been frequent but distant; now it had spurted into sudden nearness and was rapid, frequent, continuous. A little group of his fellow-toilers looked up from their work as they heard the sound, drew closer together and exchanged mutterings till an order checked them sharply; and even after the order was rapped out one square-shouldered, brown-faced countryman continued to stare down the valley with stubbornly determined eyes.

William's eyes followed the countryman's, and for a moment saw nothing but what he had seen before—cliffs, the river and the hot blue sky, without a feather of cloud to it; then, suddenly, away down the valley, there puffed out a ball of white smoke, and before it had faded another. The man with the stubborn eyes grunted something beneath his breath and turned again to his work; William, continuing to gaze curiously at the bursting puffs, was reminded of his duties by a louder shout and the threat of a lifted arm. He, too, bent again and with haste to his work; to look up furtively as the thunder deepened and see always those bursts of floating cloud down the valley or against the hot horizon.

He knew, or rather guessed, in after days when his sublime ignorance of all things military had been tempered by the newspapers, by daily war-talk and by actual contact with the soldier, that the sudden appearance of those bursting puffs had indicated some temporary and local check to the advancing German divisions, that a French or Belgian force must have pushed or fought its way across the triangular plateau between the Meuse and its tributary; must have driven before them the Germans in the act of occupying it, must have brought up their guns and commanded for the moment a stretch of the lateral valley and the line of communications along it. It was not left long in unmolested possession thereof; nearer guns answered it swiftly from all directions, from other heights and from the valley; shells whined overhead, from time to time the ground shook, and it dawned upon William, as he looked and listened, that what he saw was a battle.

At first he was more impressed by the thought than he was by the actuality—since the effects of the conflict were not in the beginning terrible. True there was something threatening in the near-by thudding of a German battery when first it made itself heard. But such harm as it inflicted was unseen by William, and for the space of an hour or so it drew no returning fire and the village stood untouched and undamaged. But as the evening drew in the thunder deepened and quickened; both sides, it would seem, had brought up reinforcements, and guns opened fire from new and unexpected places, from heights, from behind garden walls. Down the road along which William had been urged with ungentleness by Heinz a gun-team clattered and jingled at breakneck speed; it pulled up close to the railway line, not fifty yards from the spot where the prisoners were working in the shadow of a clump of young trees; the gun was placed swiftly in position, the horses were led away and after a momentary interval the men began to fire—steadily, swiftly, on the order. William watched them with his mouth wide open till reminded smartly of his idleness; they were so swift, precise and machine-like. It required an effort of the imagination to remember what they were doing.

"Killing," he said to himself, "those men are killing!" And he found himself wondering what their faces looked like while they killed? Whether they liked doing it? ...

He supposed later (when that first ignorance of things military was a little less sublime) that the firing from the immediate neighbourhood of the village had at first inflicted but little damage on the opposing forces on the heights; at any rate it remained practically unanswered till close upon sunset, the French or Belgian gunners concentrating their fire upon enemies nearer, more aggressive, or more vulnerably placed. Perhaps (he never knew for certain) they had got the better, for the time being, of those other more aggressive or more vulnerable opponents; perhaps they had received reinforcements which had enabled them to push higher up the valley or had at last been punished by a fire hitherto ineffectual; whatever the cause, as the sun grew red to the westward, a first shell screamed on to the dusty road outside the village and burst in a pother of smoke and flying clods. William heard the burst and saw the cloud rise; he was still round-eyed when another shell screamed overhead to find its billet in a garden wall a few yards behind the battery, scattering the stones thereof and splintering the boughs of an apple-tree. A shower of broken fragments came pattering about the station; William was perhaps too much stupefied by pain and weariness to understand the extent of his danger but several of his fellows stirred uneasily and two of them threw down their spades and started in headlong flight. They were brought up swiftly by the threat of a bayonet in their path; one of them came back sullenly dumb, the other whimpering aloud with a hand pressed to his face. William saw that his cheek was bleeding where a flying fragment had caught it. He was looking at the man as he nursed his torn face and bemoaned himself when a third shell struck what remained of the station roof.

William did not know whether he fell on his face instinctively or was thrown by the force of the explosion; he remembered only that as he scrambled to his feet, half-deafened and crying for help, he saw through a settling cloud of dust the disappearing backs of some three or four men who were all of them running away from him. He was seized with a mortal terror of being left alone in this torment of thunder and disaster; he believed he must be hurt, perhaps hurt to the death, and a pang of rage and self-pity went through him at the thought of his desertion by his fellows. He started after the vanishing backs, calling out to them to wait, abusing and appealing, and stumbling over ruin as he ran. The distant gunners had found their enemies' range, and he had not made half a dozen yards when he ducked to the threat of another shell that burst, as he thought, close beside him. He cringed and shivered for a moment, covering his eyes with his hands; then, finding himself uninjured, darted off at an angle, still shielding his eyes and gasping out, "God, oh God—for mercy's sake, oh God!" He knew in every fibre of his trembling body that he was about to die, and his prayer was meant not only for himself but for Griselda. As he ran on blindly, an animal wild and unreasoning, a hand caught him above the ankle and he screamed aloud with rage and terror at finding himself held fast.

"Let me go," he cried struggling; then, as the hand still gripped, bent down to wrest himself free and looked into a face that he knew—a young plump face with a budding moustache surmounted by a flat German cap. It was twisted now into a grin of agony, but all the same he recognized the face of the German boy-soldier who had dealt kindly with him that afternoon in the matter of the bottle of beer. He was lying on his back and covered from the middle downwards with a litter of broken beam and ironwork blown away from the ruin of the station. The effect of the recognition on William was curiously and instantly sobering; he was no longer alone in the hell where the ground reeled and men ran from him; he was no longer an animal wild and unreasoning, but a man with a definite human relationship to the boy lying broken at his feet. He began to lift the wreckage from the crushed legs and talked as he did so, forgetting that the wounded man in all likelihood understood not a word of his English.

"All right, I'll get it off, I'll help you. You were good to me giving me a drink, so I'll stay and help you. Otherwise I oughtn't to wait, not a minute—you see, I must look for my wife. My first duty is to her—she's my wife and I don't know where she is. But I won't leave you like this because of what you did for me this afternoon." He wrenched and tugged at the shattered and entangled wreckage till the boy shrieked aloud in his torment—the cry terrified William and he desisted, wringing his hands. "I'm sorry, I'm sorry, but I couldn't help it. God knows I didn't mean to hurt you and if I could be gentler I would, but it's so damnably, damnably heavy. Oh God, if some one would come and help me, if someone would only come! You see it's so heavy I can't move it without hurting you."

He explained and apologized to ears that heard not for the boy had fainted in his pain; his deep unconsciousness made extrication easier and William tugged again at the lumber until he had tugged it away. One of the wounded man's leg's was a wrenched and bloody mass; William shuddered at the sight, looked down stupidly at the dead white face and wondered what was to be done—then, feeling that something must at least be tried, put his arms round the inert body and strove to lift it from the ground. The only results were breathlessness on his part and a groan from the unconscious German. William dropped him instantly on hearing the groan, trembling at the idea of inflicting yet more suffering, torn by the thought of Griselda, longing to go and yet ashamed to leave the boy-soldier without aid. He might have hesitated longer but a for fresh explosion and crash of falling masonry; it was followed by a long-drawn screaming intolerable to hear—an Aie, Aie, Aie of unspeakable bodily pain. With a sudden sense of being hunted, being driven beyond endurance, William turned and shook his impotent fists in the direction of the unseen guns. "Can't you stop one moment?" he screamed idiotically, hating them and dancing with rage. "Can't you stop, you devils—you devils! Don't you see I'm only trying to help him?" If he had ever made any distinction between friend and enemy artillery, he had lost all idea of it now; the guns for the moment were a private persecution of himself, and he was conscious only of being foully and brutally bullied by monstrous forces with whom he argued and at whom he cursed and spat.

It was the sight of what had once been a horse that brought him again to his senses. His eye fell on it as he danced in his mad ineptitude at the side of the helpless German; it had been one of the team that galloped a gun down the by-road and was now a pulp of raw flesh, crushed bone, and most hideously scattered entrail. He stared for a moment at the horror, incredulous and frozen—then sickened, turned and ran from it in a passion of physical loathing.

For a minute or two he ran he knew not whither—straight ahead, anywhere to be away from the horror; then, as his shuddering sickness passed, there rushed back the thought of Griselda, and he reproached himself that he had halted even for a moment and even for a purpose of mercy; all his energies both of mind and body were turned to the finding of his wife. They must die, he was sure of it; he prayed only that they died together. The way he had taken lay outside the walled gardens between the village and the railway line; and as he ran he called her—"Griselda, Griselda!"—in a voice that he hardly caught himself, so persistent was the uproar of the guns. When he fled from the neighbourhood of the dismembered horse he had left behind him the path leading directly to the main street of the village—which it was his aim to reach since there he had last seen Griselda. Seeking another way to it, he halted when he came to a door in the wall, wrestled with the latch and flung himself angrily against it; it resisted, locked, and he ran on again, still panting out his wife's dear name. Twenty yards further on he came to another door in the wall and this time it opened to his hand.

In the garden beyond was no sign of the chaos that had overwhelmed his world since the morning. An orderly border of orderly flowers, espaliered walls and a tree or two ruddy with apples; and on a shaven plot of the greenest grass an empty basket chair with beside it a white cat reposing with her paws tucked under her chin. The white cat may have been deaf, or she may have been merely intrepid; whatever the cause her nerves were unaffected by the fury of conflict and she dozed serenely under shell-fire, the embodiment of comfortable dignity. She opened a warily observant eye when William rushed into her garden; but being a well-fed cat, and accustomed to deference, she took no further precaution. She stirred not even when he hurried past her to her dwelling-house, and as he entered it by an open window her nose descended to rest on her folded paws.

The room he ran into through the open window left no impression on the mind of William Tully; it was dark after the sunlight outside, and he supposed it must have been empty. He went rapidly along the short passage beyond it, making for the front door; he met no one, heard no one, and his fingers were touching the latch when he saw, through an open door to the right of him, the figure of a kneeling woman. She was stout, dressed in black and grey-headed and she knelt leaning on a chair in the middle of the polished floor; her eyes were closed, her lips moved, and her hands were clasped under her chin. The sound of William's feet did not reach her through the tumult of fighting without, nor did he stay to disturb her. When he lived in the world and not hell it would have seemed to him strange and unfitting that he should intrude on an old woman's privacy and secret prayer; now nothing was strange, nothing unfitting or impossible.... He supposed that she was the white cat's mistress, noted without emotion that her cheeks were wet with tears and thought vaguely that her face was familiar, that he had seen it somewhere before. Afterwards it came to him that he had seen it when the hostages died in the morning, that it was she who had prayed in the road with folded hands and pressed her crucifix to the mayor's long grey moustache. He wondered, then, what became of her and her well-fed indifferent cat.

That was afterwards, many weeks afterwards; for the time being he had no interest to give her, his thoughts were only of Griselda and the means by which she might be found. His plan, so far as it could be called a plan, was to run from house to house in the village street until he came to the place where she was captive; but when he stepped into the road it was to find it impossible of passage by reason of the men and vehicles that choked the stretch in front of him. Almost opposite the door he came through, a motor-ambulance, going eastward with its load, had collided with an ammunition wagon going west, thus bringing to a standstill more ammunition wagons and a battery of horse-artillery, its foremost ranks thrown back in confusion by a threatening skid of the ambulance. There was much whistling, and shouting of orders in the attempt to reform and clear the road; horses reared from the suddenness with which they were pulled up and men ran to their heads to steady them. While the locked wheels were wrestled with, a bandaged bloody face peered round the tail of the ambulance; the press swayed to and fro, filling the road from side to side, and William, unable to move, flattened back against the door from which he had issued, out of reach of the wicked heels of a restive horse. For the first moment he expected some one to seize and arrest him, and had he not unthinkingly closed the door behind him he would have beat a hasty retreat; but there was bloodier and busier work on hand than the corraling of stray civilians, and no man touched or questioned him as he pressed himself against the neat green-painted door. Struggling with their own most urgent concerns, not a soldier so much as noticed him; and it was borne in on William that if the wicked heels had caught him and kicked his life out, not a man would have noticed that either.

Further down the street was a cloud of slowly rising black smoke—and suddenly through it a banner of flame leaped up and waved triumphantly; one of the tidy two-storied houses had been set afire by a shell. As William watched the resplendent flare the crowd round the two vehicles composed itself into something like order, and the ambulance—its driver, by the excited movements of his mouth, still shouting out angry explanations—was backed from the path of the advancing troops and thrust crippled against the wall. The guns on one side of the road, the wagons on the other stirred forward—at first slowly, then, as the line straightened itself out, with a rattle of increasing speed. As they passed the house afire the smoke rolled down on them and hid them from William's sight.

CHAPTER X

With the conviction that no one was heeding his comings and goings, a certain amount of assurance came back to William Tully, and as the way cleared before him he set off down the street without any attempt at concealment. By house to house visitation he sought for his wife through the village; it was there she had been taken from him, and he thrust back the deadly suspicion that she need not have remained in the place where she had disappeared from his sight.

There was not a closed door in the length of the street, and nowhere was his entrance barred; the call to arms had temporarily cleared the houses of the invaders quartered in them, and he ran from one doorway to another unhindered, calling on Griselda as he entered, looking into every room, and then out to repeat the process. The two first houses were empty from garret to cellar, but with signs of having been left, recently and hurriedly, by the soldiers billeted therein; odds and ends of military kit were scattered about, chairs overturned and left lying; and in one room, a kitchen, on a half-extinguished fire, a blackened frizzle of meat in a frying-pan filled the air with a smell of burning. The third house he thought likewise empty; downstairs there was the same litter—overthrown furniture and food half eaten on the table; but opening the door of an upper room he came on a woman with three children. The woman started to her feet as the door opened, a child hugged to her bosom and other two clinging to her skirt; and William had a passing impression of a plump, pallid face with lips apart and wide, wet eyes, half-imploring and half-defiant. One of the children was crying—its mouth was rounded in a roar—but you heard nothing of its vigorous plaint for the louder din without. William made a gesture that he meant to be reassuring, shut the door and ran back into the street.

He went in and out desperately, like a creature hunted or hunting; and, having drawn blank in house after house, the deadly thought refused to be thrust and kept under. If they had taken her away, she might be ... anywhere! East or west, gone in any direction, and leaving no clue for her following. Anywhere in a blind incomprehensible world, where men killed men and might was right, and life, as he knew it from his childhood up, had ended in an orgy of devilry! He went on running from house to house, while shells screamed and burst and guns clattered by, and no man gave heed to his running or the tumult and torture of his fears. Upstairs and down and out again—upstairs and down and out.

He was nearing the end of the street when he found her at last; in the upper back room of a little white house some yards beyond the building in flames, and not far from the spot where they had seen the hostages die. She was alone and did not move when he flung the door open; crouched in a corner with her head on her knees, she neither saw nor heard him. For an instant it seemed to him that his strength would fail him for gladness, and he staggered and held to the door; as the giddiness passed he ran to her, babbling inaudible relief, and pulled the hands from her face. He had an instant's glimpse of it, white and tear-marked, with swollen lips and red eyes; then, as his arms went round her and he had her up from the floor, it went down on his shoulder and was hidden. He felt her clinging to him, trembling against him, sobbing against him while he held her—and all his soul was a passion of endearment and thankfulness.... So for a minute or two—perhaps longer—they clung to each other, reunited: until William, his sense of their peril returning, sought to urge his wife to the door.

She came with him for a step or two, her head still on his shoulder; then, suddenly, she shivered and wrestled in his arms, thrust him from her, rushed back to the end of the room and leaned against it, shaking with misery. Her arm was raised over her hidden face and pressed against the wall; and he saw what he had not seen before, that the sleeve was torn and the flesh near the wrist bruised and reddened. He saw also—his eyes being opened—that it was not only her hair that was tumbled; all her dress was disordered and awry. There was another tear under the armpit where the sleeve had given way and the white of her underlinen showed through the gap.... His heart cried out to him that she had struggled merely as a captive, had been restrained by brute force from escaping—but his own eyes had seen that she turned from him as if there was a barrier between them, as if there was something to hide that yet she wished him to know.... For a moment he fought with the certainty, and then it came down on him like a storm: for once in his life his imagination was vivid, and he saw with the eyes of his mind as clearly as with the eyes of his body. All the details, the animal details, her cries and her pitiful wrestlings; and the phrase "licentious soldiery" personified in the face of the man who had been Griselda's gaoler. Round and roughly good-humoured in repose with black eyebrows and a blue-black chin.... He caught her by the hands and said something to her— jerked out words that stammered and questioned—and she sobbed and turned her face from him again.... After that he could not remember what he felt or how long he stood in the middle of the room, oblivious of danger and staring at her heaving shoulders and the tumbled hair that covered them; but it seemed to him that he talked and moved his hands and hated—and did not know what to do.

In the end there must have come to him some measure of helpless acquiescence, or perhaps he was quieted and taken out of himself by the need of giving help to Griselda. After how long he knew not he found himself once more with his arms around her; she let him take her hand, he kissed it and stroked her poor hair. This time she came with him when he led her to the door, and they went down the stairway together. Near the street door she hesitated and halted, and he saw she had something to say.

"Where are we going?" she asked, with her lips to his ear. "Can we get away?"

He told her he thought so, that now was the time when they might slip away unnoticed—trying to encourage her by the assumption of a greater confidence than he felt. Fortune favoured them, however, and the assumption of confidence was justified; though the bombardment had slackened as suddenly as it had begun, the remnant of German soldiery left in the place was still too much occupied with its own concerns to interfere with a couple of civilians seeking safety in the rear of the fire-zone, and no one paid any heed to them as they made their way along the street. They turned inevitably westward—away from the guns—down the road they had come that morning: two hunted, dishevelled little figures, keeping well to the wall and glancing over their shoulders. The crush of wagons, of guns and men, had moved forward and out of the village, which, for the moment, seemed clear of all but non-combatants—save for the ubiquitous cyclist who dashed backwards and forwards in his dust. An ambulance was discharging its load at a building whence waved the Red Cross, and near at hand, but out of sight, a battery was thudding regularly; but of the few uniformed figures in the street itself there was none whose business it was to interest himself in their movements. They hurried on, clinging to each other and hugging the wall—except when a heap of fallen brickwork, a derelict vehicle or other obstacle forced them out into the road.

They were almost at the entry of the village when they came upon such an obstacle: the upper part of one of the endmost houses had evidently been struck by a shell, for a large slice of roof and outside wall had crumbled to the pathway below. It had crumbled but recently, since the dust was still clouding thickly above the ruin and veiling the roadway beyond it; hence, as they skirted its borders, it was not until he was actually upon them that they were aware of a motor-cyclist speeding furiously out of the dusk. The roar of the battery a few yards away had drowned the whirr of his machine, and Griselda was almost under it before she had warning of its coming. The stooping rider yelled and swerved, but not enough to avoid her; she went down, flung sideways, while the cyclist almost ran on to the heap of rubble on his right—then, recovering his balance, dashed forward and was lost in the dusk. Save for that momentary swerve and stagger, he had passed like a bolt on his errand, leaving Griselda crumpled in the road at William's feet. To his mind, no doubt, a mishap most luckily avoided. Griselda lay without moving, her face to the dust, and for one tortured moment William thought the life beaten out of her; but when he raised her, her lips moved, as if in a moan, and as he dragged her for safety to the side of the road she turned her head on his arm. He laid her down while he ran for water from the river; panted to its brim, soaked his handkerchief for lack of a cup, brought it back and pressed it to her forehead. Her eyes, when she opened them, were glazed with pain and her lips drawn tightly to her teeth; when he wanted to raise her to a sitting position she caught his hand thrust it from her and lay with her white face working. So she lay, for minutes that seemed hours, with her husband kneeling beside her.... Men passed them but stayed not; and once, when William looked up, a car was speeding by with helmeted officers inside it—too intent on their own hasty business of death to have so much as a glance to spare for a woman in agony of bodily pain and a man in agony of mind.

The night had come down before Griselda was able to move. With its fall the near-by battery was silenced and the distant thunder less frequent; so that William was able to hear her when she spoke and asked him to lift her. He sobbed for joy as he lifted her, gently and trembling lest he hurt her; she sat leaning on his arm, breathing painfully and telling him in jerks that it was her side that pained her most—her left side and her left arm, but most of all her side. At first she seemed dazed and conscious only of her sufferings—whimpered about them pitifully with intervals of silence—but after ten minutes or so she caught his sleeve and tugged it.

"Let's get away. Help me up!"

He suggested that she should rest a little longer, but she urged him with trembling, "Let's get away!" and he had perforce to raise her. In spite of the fever for flight that had taken possession of her she cried out as he helped her to her feet and stood swaying with her eyes shut and her teeth bitten hard together. He would have lain her down again, but she signed a "No, no!" at the attempt and gripped at his shoulder to steady herself; then, after a moment, guided his arm round her body, so that he could hold her without giving unnecessary pain.

"You mustn't press my side—I can't bear it. But if you put your hand on my shoulder——"

They moved away from the village at a snail's pace, Griselda leaning heavily on her husband. Behind them at first was the red light from burning houses; but as they crawled onwards the darkness of the valley closed in on them until, in the sombre shadow of the cliff, William could only distinguish his wife's face as a whitish patch upon his shoulder. When she groaned, as she did from time to time, he halted to give her relief, but she would never allow him to stand for more than a minute or two; after a few painful breaths there would come the tug of her fingers at his coat that was the sign to move forward again. Once or twice she whispered to know if any one were coming after them, and he could feel her whole body a-quiver with fear at the thought.

Barred in by cliff to right and river to left, they kept perforce to the road—or, rather, to the turf that bordered it. The traffic on the road itself had not ceased with the falling of night; cars were coming up and guns were coming up and the valley was alive with their rumble—and at every passing Griselda shrank and her fingers shivered in their grip upon William's sleeve.

"Can't we get away from them?" she whispered at last. "Right away and hide—can't we turn off the road?"

He said helplessly that he did not know where, until they reached the entrance to their valley. "It's all cliff—and the river on the other side."

She had known it without asking; there was nothing for it but to drag herself along. To both the distance was never-ending; Griselda's terror of recapture communicated itself to her husband, and he shivered even as she did at the rattle of a passing car. Instinctively they kept to the shadow, stumbling in its blackness over the uneven ground below the cliff. Once, when a couple of patrolling horsemen halted near them in the roadway, they crouched and held their breath during an eternity of dreadful seconds while they prayed that they had not been noticed. It seemed to William that his heart stopped beating when one of the horsemen walked his beast a yard or two nearer and flashed a light into their faces; but the man, having surveyed them, turned away indifferently and followed his comrade down the road. That was just before they came to the gap in the heights that led into the valley of silence.

As they entered it for the last time, in both their minds was the thought that they might find it barred to them; and the beating of their hearts was loud in their ears as they crept into its friendly shadow.

"The woods," Griselda whispered.

They turned into the woods and took cover; and, with a yard or two, the blackness under the trees had closed in on them, blotting out all things from sight. They halted because they could see to walk no further.

"Let me down," Griselda said—and her husband knew by the gasp in her voice that she was at the end of her powers of endurance. He explored with an outstretched hand for a tree trunk and lowered her gently to the ground with her back supported against it; she panted relief as he sat down beside her and groped for her fingers in the darkness.... So they sat holding to each other and enveloped in thickest night.

The guns had died down altogether, and the rumble from the road, though almost continuous was dulled—so that William could hear his wife's uneven breathing and the stealthy whisper of the trees. He sat holding Griselda's hand and staring into the blackness, a man dazed and confounded; who yesterday was happy lover and self-respecting citizen and to-day had suffered stripes, been slave and fugitive, learned the evil wrought on his wife.

Thinking on it afterwards, he wondered that he had closed an eye; yet he had sat in the darkness but a very few minutes when, swiftly and without warning, he fell into a heavy sleep.

CHAPTER XI

He woke with the blaze of the eastern sun in his eyes, and on the first sensation of bewilderment at finding his bed was moss, came a rush of remembrance and with it self-reproach—he had slept while Griselda suffered. He knelt and bent over her as she lay still asleep, huddled on her right side; her face was flushed, her lips were cracked, and she was breathing in heavy little snorts. As he knelt and gazed the thunder of yesterday broke out in the distance, and Griselda stirred and woke moaning.

Her first cry was for water, and in the insistence of her thirst she was oblivious of everything but her burning need to slake it; he broke cover and ran to the stream, some fifty yards away, soaked his handkerchief and made a tight cup of his hands. The cup was a failure, and the little that was left in it when he reached Griselda was spilled when she tried to drink; but the dripping handkerchief she sucked at eagerly and gave back for another soaking. He was about to break cover to wet it again when he caught sight first of one, then of half-a-dozen horsemen entering the valley by the gap; and shrank back, cowering, into the friendly shelter of the tree-trunks—sick with uncertainty as to whether or no they had seen him. He judged not when he saw them dismount and picket their horses; and having watched them long enough to see that they were making preparations for a meal, he turned and crept back to Griselda.

The terror of yesterday came down on her when she heard his whispered news. A moment before she had seemed incapable of movement, lain crumpled on her side and repulsed, with a feverish pettishness, his efforts to stir and raise her; now she clung to him and struggled to her feet, even pain forgotten in the passion for instant flight. So, holding together, they fled again: fled crawling, they knew not whither. Two instincts guided them and directed their stumbling footsteps: the instinct to leave far behind them the threat of the guns and the instinct to keep out of sight. Thus they held to the woods above the valley of silence, avoiding all paths that led out into the open; their direction, roughly, was southward—though they did not know it—and they dragged a mile, or even less, where a man in health might make five.

When they had gone some few hundred yards they struck the trickle of a hill-side rivulet on its way to join the stream in the valley. At the sound of its babble Griselda cried out and tried to hasten, and, when they came to it, slipped down till she could thrust her face into the water and drink like the sun-parched Israelites who marched with Gideon. They drank, they dabbled in it, bathed hands and feet, and Griselda washed her broken side—touching it gingerly and not daring to pull away the linen that the blood had caked to the flesh. After that William helped her to her feet and they dragged on further.

If they found water in abundance, they found but little to eat; and though Griselda made no complaint of hunger, as the hours went by it gnawed at her husband's vitals. At first their path lay chiefly through beechwoods bare of undergrowth, and they had been an hour or two on their way before they came to blackberry bushes. Upon these William fell, tearing his hands on the thorns by his eager stripping of the bushes; Griselda would hardly touch them, but he shovelled them into his mouth and ate long and voraciously. He had toiled much the day before and eaten little—a scanty breakfast and the scraps of bread and meat allotted by his captors at midday—and, shovel as he might, the berries were a poor substitute for the meal he craved and dreamed of. That was a meal which floated before the eye of his mind as phantom ham and eggs, phantom cuts from the joint, thick slabs of well-buttered bread; something solid that a man could set his teeth in and gnaw till his stomach was satisfied. He was ashamed of the way in which food and the longing for food possessed him—so that there were moments when the phantom joint was more present to his mind than Griselda or the fear of death itself.

To the phase of violent and savage hunger succeeded, with hours, a giddy dreaminess, the result of growing exhaustion. As the day wore on and exhaustion increased, his mind, like his body, refused to work connectedly; his feet often stumbled and he was incapable of consecutive thought. Once he found himself sitting with Griselda under a beech-tree, holding her fingers and considering how they had come there and why they had got to go on; and wandering off into vague recollection of the story of a knightly lover who had carried his mistress long miles through a forest in his arms. The details of the story escaped his memory and he sought for them with pettish insistence; with perhaps at the back of his mind some idea, born of brain-fag, that, did he but remember them, he could do the same service for Griselda.

He had soon lost all sense of direction; but the instinct to hide never left him, and once or twice, when the wood seemed to be opening out, he drew his wife back to the solitude under the trees. With the passing of the hours their rests by the way grew longer; Griselda was able to keep her feet for a few minutes only before she muttered or signed a request for another halt. Whereat William would lower her to the ground where she propped herself against a tree-trunk or lay huddled and silent with closed eyes.

At one such halt he fell suddenly and helplessly asleep; perhaps Griselda did the same, for though the sun was high when he sat him down the woods were heavy with blue dusk when she roused him by a tugging at his sleeve. She was craving again for water; her lips were cracked for the want of it. They rose and went blindly in search—halting every few minutes as much to strain their ears for the longed-for ripple as to give Griselda strength. More than once she was at failing point; so much so that he suggested she should lie down while he hunted further for a stream. She refused, trembling at the idea of being left alone—unreasonably, but perhaps wisely, since William, astray in the darkening woods, might well have had difficulty in finding his way to her again.

The dusk was more than dusk before they found what they sought; it was actual darkness of night descending to cover the earth. They had halted perforce more than once when Griselda could go no further; but always her thirst burned her, and she rose and struggled forward again. She was past speaking when they came on a clearing, and then on a stream that ran through it, of which they were only aware when they trod into the marshy ground at its brim. She drank heavily, lay inert and seemed to sleep.

Perhaps because he had slept for so long in the afternoon her husband was more wakeful; for hours he sat with his eyes wide and his chin propped on his hands. After nightfall had come silence from the guns and at first the only sounds were forest sounds—night-bird talk and the lapping of unseen water at his feet. Later Griselda was restless and became conversational, talking rapidly and brokenly in a delirium of pain and fever and paying no heed to his efforts to answer and calm her. Her mind, uncontrolled, had returned to a familiar channel; she was back in the world that had crumbled but yesterday, waging war as she understood it till she saw the hostages die. The Great Civil War that you fought with martyrdoms, with protests at meetings and hammers on plate-glass windows—he could hear she was back in the thick of it incoherently addressing an audience. Snatches of old-time denunciation—Asquith, McKenna, the sins of the Labour Party—and, emerging from a torrent of incomprehensibility, the names of the Leaders of the Movement. He listened, crouched in the darkness, a starving fugitive—who had seen men dismembered and done to death in a war that was not civil; and suddenly, crouched and starving in the darkness, he began to laugh out loud. He remembered—quite plainly he remembered—a letter written to the daily Press to point out with indignation that one of the Leaders of the Movement had been hurt in the ankle in the course of the Great Civil War.... He only laughed briefly; the echo of his own voice frightened him, and its cackle died swiftly away. In the grave black silence it sounded like a blasphemy, and he told himself excusingly that he had not been able to help it.

With rest and cessation of movement his brain worked more easily; and with the passing of his first savage hunger he was no longer preoccupied with the needs of his empty stomach. He considered the situation, dispassionately and curiously detached from it; deciding, with an odd lack of emotion, that to-morrow could not be as to-day. Whatever the need, Griselda could walk no further; he, for his part, was incapable of dragging her; when the light came they must just sit and wait. His mind refused to trouble itself with details of what would happen if they sat and waited too long. Looking back at that night it seemed to him that he was not able to feel very much; his capacity for emotion was exhausted, even as his body. When Griselda stirred or groaned he tried to shift her more comfortably, when she gasped for water he helped her to bend down and drink; but the power of imaginative terror had left him for the time being, and he no longer trembled and sickened at her suffering as he had done when she was first struck down.

He fell into a doze in the last hours of night, and when his eyes opened the sky was a pearly grey. He could see a wide stretch of it over the tree-tops; for at the spot to which they had wandered in the uncertainty of darkness the grouping of the trees was less close than it had been, and there was a suggestion of open space beyond them. Griselda lay sleeping or unconscious, with her knotted hair straying on her face; he smoothed it away as he knelt beside her, took her hand and called her by name. She gave no answer, and did not even stir when he kissed her. The power of imaginative terror had returned to him, and he asked himself whether she were dying? ... He knelt beside her for a few minutes, fondling her hand and whispering, imploring her to speak—and then, in a mingled curse and appeal, stretched his arms above his head towards heaven. The effort and emotion exhausted him; he collapsed both bodily and mentally, slipped back to the grass beside his wife and lay with his face to the ground.

What roused him was the sound of a man's voice near him; not words, but a grunt of surprise unmistakably human. He lifted his head and saw gazing at him from the opposite bank of the brook the man who had uttered the grunt. A man carrying a pail, very filthy and many days unshorn; with a peaked cap flattened on the back of his head, a dark muddied coat and loose trousers that had once been red. His face, for all its grime and its black sprouts of beard, was reassuring in its interest; what he said was gibberish to

William's ears, but the sound of it kindly and inquiring, and, when William shook his head and pointed to his wife, he set down his unfilled pail on the grass and waded across the shallow stream. He looked at Griselda, touched her torpid hand gently and muttered more friendly gibberish; finishing by a pat on William's shoulder before he waded back to the further bank, filled his pail to the brim and walked away with it. He turned to fling back a last gesture of promise before he vanished among the trees, leaving William to stare after him, motionless and dumb, and waiting for something, he knew not what, to happen.

What happened, after an interval, was the reappearance of the pail-bearer, this time minus his pail, but accompanied, in its stead, by a comrade. The comrade was scarcely less filthy and similarly clad; the twain emerged from between the trees, splashed across the brook and exchanged rapid gibberish while they stood and looked down at Griselda. Finally, one of them, addressing himself to William, pointed to somewhere on the opposite bank and nodded with intent to encourage; whereupon the pair of them lifted Griselda, made a seat of their arms and carried her. William followed them, lurching from weakness as he walked; and after they had gone about a couple of hundred yards the little procession came out on to a highway where a hooded car, as dirty as its guardians, was drawn up at the side of the road.

On the floor of the car the two men placed Griselda, laying her down gently and arranging, with kind, dirty hands, some empty sacks as a makeshift couch and a coat as a makeshift pillow. That done, they signed to William to climb in beside his wife, and one of them, noticing his feebleness, lent a hand to him over the tailboard, while the other provided him with a hunk of bread and a large tin mug of red wine. His hunger returned with the taste of food, and he ate with a ravenous enjoyment, gulping down bread and wine together; before he had finished gulping the car had started and was rattling over the road, he knew not whither. Woods went by them and open spaces; they spanned rivers, climbed hills and descended again into valleys. Sometimes the roads were rough, and at the jolting of the car Griselda would whimper and cry out—whereat William would try to soothe her with assurance that the worst was over, they were safe and would soon be in comfort. He did not know if she understood; she never spoke coherently and hardly ever opened her eyes.

For the first wooded mile or two they had the road to themselves; after that they came across other traffic, the greater part of it heading in the same, mostly southerly, direction. It was varied traffic, mechanical, horse and foot: guns and other cars, some signed with the Geneva cross; now a cavalry patrol, now a dusty detachment of infantry; and, intermingled with soldier stragglers, little groups of non-military wayfarers, in carts and tramping afoot. All these grew more frequent as the miles went under them; so frequent as to hinder their progress, and finally, when they neared their destination, bring the pace of the car to a crawl.

Their destination—William never knew its name—was a white-walled village, whereof the one long street was crowded with the traffic of humanity; the same kind of traffic they had passed on the road, but thickened and impeded by much that was stationary in horses, in men and in vehicles. The car jolted half-way along the stone-paved street and came to a standstill in the company of three or four others; its guardians descended and one of them—the pail-bearer—looked over the tail and nodded in friendly-wise to William before he hurried away. There was a few minutes' wait, during which nothing personal happened—only the confused sound of voices, the confused sound of movement flowing incessantly, movement of feet, wheels and engines; and then the man who had nodded from the tail of the car came back, others with him—dirty soldiers like unto himself. One of these spoke to William, choosing his words with precision; and when he shook his head and answered, "I am English," there was talk and much gesticulation. (It struck him later that they took him for a Flemish-speaking Belgian and perhaps had tried him with a word or two of the language.) To the accompaniment of talk and gesticulation the tailboard of the car was let down and William, by sign, was invited to set foot on the ground; whereafter Griselda was also lifted out and laid by the roadside on a truss of hay which some one had procured for the purpose. There she lay for another ten minutes or so, unaware of her surroundings while the stream of humanity flowed by her—William, hunched beside her on the hay, wondering dumbly what would happen to them next. He knew himself among friends and was no longer afraid; but all initiative had left him, all power of action and idea. He had a dull hope that some one was bringing a doctor ... meanwhile he could do nothing but wait and obey, and when his good Samaritan, the filthy little soldier, came back and tapped him on the shoulder, he rose, passively responsive.

The man signed to him that they should lift Griselda between them; he obeyed with infinite difficulty, panting at the effort, and together they carried her some yards down the street to a cart that stood pulled up and waiting—a long, most un-English-looking country cart with a man perched in front and inside two women, many bundles, some ducks and a goat. One of the women was shrivelled and helpless with years; her head in a handkerchief and her gnarled fingers holding to her knees, she sat huddled against the protesting goat, a lump of bent, blear-eyed old age. Her companion in discomfort—possibly her daughter—was a stout, elderly peasant woman, the counterpart in petticoats of the grizzled-haired man who guided a solid grey farmhorse. She made room for Griselda, talking rapidly the while, in the straw at the bottom of the cart—thrusting ducks and bundles to one side of the vehicle with her knotted and energetic hands; perhaps she was striving to explain to William that it was impossible to accommodate another passenger and that he must follow on foot. She may have been friend or acquaintance of the dirty Samaritan, for, as the cart moved off at a foot's pace, she waved to him in friendly guise; the dirty Samaritan, for his part, clapping William on the back, pointing after the cart and showing his teeth in a final grin of encouragement. In the days that followed William often regretted that he had not known how to thank him for the bounty of his overflowing charity.

He walked after the cart as it lumbered through the village and out of it. Nourishment and the sense of relief had given back some of his strength; thus he was able, if with difficulty, to keep up with the plodding of the solid grey farmhorse—often brought to a standstill, moreover, by the traffic that cumbered the road. Sometimes the standstill was a long one, accompanied by confusion and shouting; there was a point where a stream of fugitives flowing southward met reinforcements hurrying north—and a flock of panic-stricken sheep, caught between the two, charged backwards and forwards, to the yells of their sweating drivers and the anger of a captain of cavalry. At almost every cross-roads the stream was swollen by a fresh rivulet of fugitives—refugees human and animal; thus at such junctions the pace was slower and a halt frequently called for. When it came William dropped down with thankfulness; sometimes lying torpid till the cart moved on, sometimes satisfying hunger and quenching thirst with fruit from the regiments of orchard trees that lined the sides of the road.

The stout peasant woman was more kindly than a hard face promised. She was careful and troubled about many things—the old wreck of humanity, her live-stock, the safety of herself and her bundles—and she had lost her home and her livelihood; but she found time to think of Griselda and do what she could for her. She arranged her straw pillow, wiped the dust from her face, and from time to time raised her that she might hold a cup to her lips. Somewhere about midday she attended to the general needs; the cart was halted and she doled out a ration all round—hunks of bread chopped from a yard of loaf and portions of a half-liquid cheese. William was not forgotten, and shared with the rest of the party; they ate with the cart drawn up in a field a little way from the road; the horse grazing, the goat tethered to one of the wheels, the peasants and William sitting on the ground and Griselda lying in her straw. William climbed up beside her and coaxed a little wine between her lips; she had swallowed hardly a mouthful when she turned her head aside and pushed the mug feebly away. He was not sure if she responded when he spoke to her and stroked her hand; she muttered once or twice but it was only a sound to his ears. For a moment—perhaps it was the raw, red wine that had mounted to his head—there came over him a sort of irritation at her long and persistent silence. She must know what it meant to see her suffer and have no word; he felt she might have tried to rouse herself to the extent of one little smile of comfort.

The afternoon was as the morning—a weary journeying whereof he knew not the goal. The grey horse plodded, the women sat hunched amid their bundles, and William tramped on his blistered feet at the tail of the creaking cart; when he looked ahead the road, as far as his eye could reach, was dotted with fugitive tramps and fugitive vehicles—and when he looked back there were others following in their tracks. For the most part, however, he looked neither back nor forward but trudged with his eyes on the ground through the whitened grass at the roadside. No rain had fallen for many days and the road was deep in dust; it hung heavy in the air and when a car went by it rose in clouds like smoke. The trees were thick with it, and every man's garments were powdered by its uniform grey.

More than once their way led them through a village—which might have been always the same village, so alike was its aspect and its doings. Always some of the houses would be closed and some in the act of emptying; in each and all was the same scene of miserable haste, of loading carts, of families, scared and burdened, setting out on their flight to the southward. It was a scene that grew so familiar to William that, staggering with the weight of his own weariness, he hardly turned his head to watch it; it affected him only by the halts it caused, by the need of manoeuvring through a crowd. Cut off from his fellows by the lack of intelligible speech, he trudged on like an animal at the tail of the cart, ignorant as an animal of what the next hours might bring him.

There were moments when it seemed to him that he was asleep and would surely waken; when he put out his hand to touch something and feel that it resisted and was real—a dusty axle, a gate, a wall, the dusty bark of a fruit-tree. And there were other moments when the *now* was real, and he seemed to have newly wakened from the dream of a world impossible—of streets and stations and meals that came regularly, of life that was decent and reasonable and orderly, with men like unto himself.... Late in the afternoon he started and lifted his head in sudden trembling recognition of a sound reminiscent, and because reminiscent beloved—the near-by whistle of a passing engine, the near-by clank of a train. The note of the whistle, the sight of a long line of trucks—but a field's-breadth away behind a fence—brought a rush of hope to his heart and a rush of tears to his eyes. His soul thrilled with the promise of them; after the vagabond horror of the last few days they stood for decency, for civilization, for a means of escape from hell. His eyes followed the train with longing as it snorted over a level meadow and wound out of sight behind a hill—followed it with longing, with something that was almost love.

A mile or two further they passed a level crossing and soon after came again on a village. It was larger than any they had so far traversed, and in ordinary times must have been of a prosperous importance; now many of its windows were bolted and shuttered, denoting the flight of inhabitants whom others were preparing to follow. The sun was red in the west when they reached its outskirts.

It was when they were about halfway along the wide paved street that there came a loud cry from the cart—so loud and so sudden that the driver pulled at his horse.

The cry had come from the hard-faced peasant woman who was leaning over Griselda. The life in William stood still as he saw her face, and she had to beckon to him twice before he moved to climb into the cart; she gave him a hand as he climbed and half jerked him over the bundles.... Griselda had died very quietly in the straw at the bottom of the cart.

CHAPTER XII

Some one, he thought, kept him back from the body while they lifted it down from the cart; there was a stir and bustle and three or four people gathered round, hiding it for a moment from his sight. One, he remembered, had the goat by the horns and was trying to drag it aside; the goat was refractory, kicked and bleated and made itself the centre of a scuffle. Afterwards he pushed through them all and stood looking down at his wife.

As he looked at her—limp, with glazed eyes and fallen jaw—there swam before his memory a pitiful vision of the dear Griselda he had married. He saw her—this huddle of rags and dirt—in her wedding garments, fussed and dainty, with her bouquet tied with suffragette ribbons. He remembered the expression, self-conscious and flushing, wherewith she had given her hand that he might place the ring on her finger; and how, when they were first alone as man and wife, he had taken the hand that wore the ring and kissed it till she drew it away. The crowd in the little house at Balham, the handshakes, the well-wishing faces—they were all so close and so present that they gave the lie to this dead woman dropped by the roadside. He looked down stupidly while the bystanders whispered and stared.

He did not know how long he sat beside her, nursing a dead hand in his own; but he knew he hated and shrank from the people around him—a group that kept forming and moving away and whispering as it gazed at himself and the body of his wife. It was a changing little crowd, never more than a dozen or so; men and women who stopped in their passing by, muttered questions, heard low answers, looked curious or pitying and moved on. He hated its inquisitiveness, he shrank from its pity, desiring to be alone with his dead. That he might not see its curious and pitying faces he pressed a hand over his eyes.

After some time—either minutes or hours—came a hand on his shoulder that stayed till he moved and looked up. He who had touched him wore the garb of a priest; was stout, not over-well washed or brushed, but kindly of manner and countenance. He spoke while the crowd stared and listened; William moved his head irritably, muttered, "I can't understand what you say," and would have covered his eyes again if he had not heard an English voice beside him. It was a woman who had caught his words and now pushed through the bystanders: a tall young woman in tweed coat and skirt, who had stayed to look over the shoulders of the shifting group.

"You are English?" she said. "What has happened?" He stared up at her for a moment, amazed at the sound of his own tongue.

"My wife is dead," he told her; and, hearing himself say the words aloud, he burst into a passion of sobbing. Through it he choked incoherent appeals to "take them away—for God's sake to let him be alone." He turned his face to the wall and wept, long and brokenly, as one who has nothing more to hope; and for a time they left him till the paroxysm should wear itself out.

When he turned his head at last the crowd that he hated had scattered; perhaps the priest and the Englishwoman had persuaded it away, for they were the only two near him. The Englishwoman, with her hands thrust deep into the pockets of her tweed coat, was standing at his shoulder, waiting till he was ready to listen.

"Will you come with me?" she asked. "It will be better." Her tone, though very gentle, was authoritative and brought him instinctively to his feet; but once there he hesitated to follow her and stammered that he could not leave— —

"It will only be for a moment. The priest—he will see—he will bring her."

She put a hand on his arm and led him unresisting down the street—a hundred yards or so, past the church and into a house standing back from the road in a garden. He knew afterwards that it was the village presbytery and that the little woman who moved aside from the garden gate to let them pass in was the priest's elderly housekeeper. His companion spoke to her in French, no doubt to explain their arrival; and the old woman trotted ahead to the house, opened a door to the right and ushered them into a sitting-room that smelt of unopened window. It was a ceremonious as well as a stuffy little room; there were good books lying on a table in the centre and stiff chairs ranged against the walls. Having offered them a couple of the stiff-backed chairs the housekeeper withdrew to her vigil at the garden gate; William sat where she had placed him, but the Englishwoman walked to the window.

"I wish I could help you," she said with her back towards him. "I know nothing seems any good at such a time, but if there is anything you want— —"

She was giving him more than she knew by her presence, by speaking in their common tongue; the sound of the familiar, comprehensible English was as the breaking of an iron barrier between him and the rest of mankind. She was talking to him—talking, not mouthing and making strange noises. He was back in the world where you spoke and your fellows understood you, where you were human—intelligent, intelligible—not an animal guided by nod and beck or driven to labour by blows. Comprehensible speech meant not only sympathy, but the long-denied power of complaint—and the pent and swollen misery of his last few days was relieved by a torrent of words. She stood and listened while he sobbed and talked incoherently. There was small plan or sequence about his tale—he went backwards and forwards in it, started afresh and left gaps; but she realized that he was telling it not for her benefit, but for his own relief, let him pour himself out and refrained from interruption even when his talk was most entangled. She took it as a good sign when at last he paused and looked up to ask of her what it all meant, what had happened, and where he was now?

She told him, as briefly as might be, what Heinz had told him—of a world in upheaval and nations at grips with each other; the same story if not from the same point of view. She added that he was now on French soil (which he had not guessed) some miles from the Belgian frontier, and that it would be possible, she hoped, to make the journey onward by rail. The French were falling back and the district had been warned of the likelihood of enemy occupation; she supposed that the needs of the army had absorbed the local rolling-stock, for there had been no passenger train on their small branch line that day. The authorities, however, had promised one to Paris in the morning and she, herself, was waiting in the hope of obtaining a seat. She hesitated and broke off at the sound of shuffling feet in the passage outside—slow feet and uncertain, as of men who carried a burden. William heard the sound likewise and, guessing its meaning, would have risen and gone to the door; but she kept him to his seat with a hand on his shoulder and he obeyed the touch because, at the moment, it was easier to obey than to resist. He sat and trembled, twisting his fingers, while the shuffling died away into momentary silence, followed by trampling and the closing of a door as the burden-bearers went out.... Then silence again, a much longer silence, till the stout priest entered the room, moving quietly, as men are accustomed to move in the neighbourhood of those whom no sound can arouse or disturb. He spoke softly at some length to the Englishwoman, who, having listened and nodded, turned to William and told him that if he would like to go to her— —

He followed the priest down the passage to a room at the back of the house; wherein, on a table, and covered by a sheet, they had laid the body of his wife. There were long candles burning around the table and on either side of her a little metal vase filled with roses. The priest stood aside in the doorway for William to enter, bowed his head in a prayer and went out; when he had gone William crept to the table, turned the sheet from her face and looked down—on Griselda dowered with a grave dignity that had never been hers while she lived.... Some one had washed away the stains of the road and arranged the disordered rags that had once been a dress; the hair was smoothed out of its three-day tangle and her poor hands crossed on her breast.

He stayed with her till dusk had thickened into darkness, sometimes standing at her side to look down on her face, sometimes bowed to his knees by the burden of the years without her. When the priest came back to rouse him he was crouched in the attitude of prayer; but his prayer (if such it might be called) was only the eternal petition of the bereaved, "Would God that I had died instead!"

The village sexton was of those who had already fled at the rumour of the oncoming German; so that night the Englishwoman, who had acquired in a west-country garden some skill in the handling of a spade, took turns with a bent old peasant in digging a grave for Griselda. When daylight failed them they dug by the shine of a lantern; the Englishwoman was not over-imaginative or nervous but she found the job an eerie one—the more so since the square-walled cemetery, like French graveyards in general, lay well away from its village—and she was glad when the moment came to pay off her companion and return to her quarters in the little Hôtel de la Gare. Other formalities in connection with the funeral there were none—for the reason that the maire and his clerk, who in ordinary seasons would have devoted much time and stationery to the subject, had departed that evening, bearing with them the archives of the commune.

William, for his part, spent the night on the priest's horsehair sofa, next door to the room where the candles burned around the body of his wife. From weariness of the flesh he dozed now and again; but for the greater part of the night lay wakeful and staring at darkness. There were moments when the horsehair sofa shook beneath his sobbing; and there were others when it seemed to him impossible that a horror so brutal and so undeserved should have mangled his harmless life. At one such moment he crept from his couch, felt his way across the room and into the passage—possessed by some wild and unconfessed thought that he might not find Griselda on the sheeted table with her hands crossed over her breast. The door, when he tried it, was locked and the key withdrawn—fastened by the priest or his housekeeper before they retired for the night; but when he knelt down to peer through the keyhole he could see two of the tall church candles and the vase with its bunch of white roses that some one had placed near her head. He crept back, knowing that she lay there indeed, and sat down to stare at the darkness till it softened from black into grey.

The morning was still flushed in the east when the old woman came to him with bread and a bowl of coffee; the coffee was hot, aromatic and sweet, after the fashion of that which had once been brewed by Madame Peys—and, remembering breakfasts not eaten alone, his tears dropped into it thickly. While he ate, sitting humped on the edge of the horsehair sofa, the street outside was already astir with traffic, nomad and military; those fugitives who had rested in the village for the night were once more taking to the road, other fugitives from the neighbourhood were dribbling in to join them, troops were moving up and to-day was even as yesterday. When he had finished his bread and coffee the old woman signed him to the kitchen sink, where she furnished him with soap and a towel; and, the process of washing completed, she produced a clothes-brush, led him out into the garden and attacked with vigour the mud and stain on his garments. He was standing passively while she scoured at his shoulders when the Englishwoman came up, and, looking anywhere except at his face, put his wife's rings into his hands. There were two of them—the new gold band, with a month's wear behind it, and the little engagement half-hoop—and at sight of them the housekeeper ceased to scour and crept away with her brush. He looked down at them lying in his palm till the tears veiled them, and knotted them slowly and tightly in a corner of his handkerchief. His companion cleared her throat and, still looking anywhere except at his face, told him that the train to Paris—very probably the last one to run—would be starting that morning.

"Yes?" he said vaguely, conscious that she expected a reply.

She explained that what she had meant was, the funeral must take place immediately.... Chiefly for the sake of breaking the silence she supposed that his wife was not a Roman Catholic?

He answered "No," staring at a row of hollyhocks and a butterfly that quivered above them.

She asked, she explained, because in that case the priest would have read the proper service. As it was ... She hoped he would understand that they had done their best to—be reverent. But there were difficulties—so many of the tradesmen were leaving or had left already. Carpenters and so on.... He listened stupidly with his eyes on the quivering butterfly, dumbly rebellious at the cruelty that tore him even from the body—and it only dawned on him what she meant by her stumbling hints when she led him through the house to the front door where a cart stood waiting with the priest at the horse's head. It was a farm-cart, borrowed by the priest from a neighbour; and on the floor of it that which had been Griselda lay coffinless and wrapped in a sheet. There were roses scattered on the folds of the sheet and the old Frenchwoman was waiting at the gate with a shapeless little wreath of her own manufacture which she pressed into William's hand.

They set out, a funeral procession of three, which at other times would have drawn many curious glances; the priest leading the horse and William and the Englishwoman walking side by side at the rear of the cart. The cemetery lay outside the village, a half-mile or so from their starting-point, and they passed wayfarers enough on the road, of whom some bared their heads and crossed themselves, and others were too busy with their own sorrows to give even a thought to the dead. The gate of the graveyard was narrow and it was with difficulty that the cart was manoeuvred between its posts. At an ordinary funeral the hearse would have remained in the road; but this was no ordinary funeral nor ordinary day, and it was as well not to tempt the footsore fugitive by the sight of a vehicle unguarded. Accordingly, the cart was manoeuvred through the gate before the priest, William and the Englishwoman lifted out the body of Griselda and carried it to the grave in the corner. The bent-backed old labourer was sitting beside it on the mound that would shortly fill it; he rose when he saw them, leaning on his spade and bared his grey hairs to the dead.

The grave was shallow—but, shallow as it was, the body, being coffinless, was lowered with difficulty and the Englishwoman led William a little way aside that he might not watch while the priest and the peasant performed the last service Griselda would require of man; he understood what she meant and stood with his back to the group round the grave, staring at a granite tombstone bedizened with massive bead wreaths. When she touched him on the shoulder, as sign that he might turn, the priest was crossing himself at his prayers and the old man standing by the heap of new turned earth. He went to the edge of the grave, looked down at the crumpled sheet and then stupidly round at his neighbour. He said nothing, but she thought he was expecting something; so, as the priest still prayed with closed eyes in silence, she struggled with the racial shyness where things of the spirit are concerned and, swallowing her tears, spoke the funeral words for Griselda.

"I am the Resurrection and the Life, saith the Lord: he that believeth in Me, though he were dead, yet shall he live..."

"Blessed are the dead that die in the Lord ... they rest from their labours."

"Man that is born of woman hath but a short time to live ... He cometh up and is cut down..."

"Lord have mercy upon us!"

It was all she could remember; and when William had whispered Amen they left the old peasant to his work.

CHAPTER XIII

At the gate of the cemetery they parted from the priest, who had charged himself with the immediate return of the haycart which he had borrowed from a neighbouring farm; he shook hands with them, nodded kindly to the Englishwoman's thanks, climbed into the cart and drove off along the dusty road. They saw him no more and often wondered what became of him when the wave of Teutonic invasion swept over his parish and himself. Their own way lay in the opposite direction—first back to the village inn, where the Englishwoman picked up her bag and a package of provisions for the journey, and then on to the station to await the arrival of the train. William followed her incuriously, without question or comment; and when she broke silence to explain what they were doing he assented, speaking with an effort and hardly knowing to what he assented.

The train to Paris had been announced by the station authorities for an early hour in the morning, but morning dragged on and became afternoon before it put in an appearance. They waited through long and shadeless hours—till two o'clock and after—at the most insignificant of railway stations with a crowd of would-be passengers; a crowd that swelled as the hours crawled on until it flowed from the platform far along the line, and it seemed doubtful if any train, however capacious, could absorb its swarming multitude. It sat in families about the platform and camped and shifted as an untidy fringe to the track; it was querulous, weeping, apathetic—it was also, in patches, malodorous. At midday it picknicked, squalidly enough, out of bottles and bulging handkerchiefs, finding momentary distraction in the process; for the rest it had nothing to do but exchange its miseries, stare at the curve which the train must round, listen uneasily to the echo of artillery and assail the station-master with complaining queries whenever he dared to show his face. For the most part that hapless and harried official—whose subordinates had been reft from him by mobilization and who was only too conscious that his time-table was a snare and a mockery—lay low in his miniature office; whence he peered out now and again to make anxious estimate of the numbers that blackened and overflowed his platform. As time went on and the throng grew denser, he gave up his attempts to reconcile the extent of the crowd with the cubic capacity of a highly problematical train, and retiring to his sanctum, in despair and for good, locked the door on intrusion and complaint.

Whenever—as happened not once, but often—an engine was sighted rounding the curve to the northward, there was instant bustle and expectation on the part of the waiting multitude. Makeshift luggage was collected and clutched at, mothers screamed to their straying young families and herded them together in anxious preparation for the formidable struggle ahead; but not once but often the alarm was a false one, the preparations in vain, as the train sped by without halt. The first to run past was a Red Cross train with bandaged men showing at the windows; as it slid between the platforms the crowd buzzed its disappointment and then—with the exception of some few determined souls who vented their annoyance in raps on the station-master's door—settled down in dejection to continue its weary waiting. Another half-hour of sweltering impatience and again the mothers screamed and rounded up their families, with the same result as before; this time the relentless and undelaying train was packed, not with wounded soldiers, but with refugees from higher up the line—like unto themselves but more fortunate. It was packed to the doors and beyond the doors—since men were hanging on the footboards.

For many reasons William and his guardian avoided the platform where the crowd was thickest and sat under the hedge by the line. During the first hour or two of their weary sojourn she judged him past rousing and left him to his own thoughts; and he sat by her side with his hands hugging his knees and seemingly unconscious of her presence. Later, about midday, when she fed him from the store of provisions she had brought for the journey, she essayed to rouse him by telling him how she had come there and who she was. Her name was Haynes, Edith Haynes; she had been some weeks in the neighbourhood, staying in the country house of some distant French cousins. They had been warned, soon after hostilities broke out, that proximity to the frontier might be dangerous, but had been unable to leave owing to the illness of one of the family. Yesterday the invalid, partially recovered, had been got off with her mother in a car procured with difficulty; as it had other occupants and could not carry the whole party, she—Miss Haynes—had volunteered to remain behind and follow to Paris by rail. William listened, occasionally nodding to show that he listened; in a way he was grateful for her presence, but nothing seemed to matter ... and, seeing that it was as yet too early to help him to other thoughts, she left him again to his silence.

It was after two when a nearing train slowed down as it reached the station—slowed down and came to a standstill to a tumult of pushing and shouting. It was a train of more than ordinary dimensions—a couple of engines to an interminable line of third-class carriages and vans—but long as it was, it was none too long for the needs of the would-be passengers. Vans and carriages alike were already well stocked with humanity; but the other humanity on the platform, rendered desperate by its waiting, hurled itself at the doors and pressed and fought a way in. The sight was not pleasant—there was trampling, expostulation, threats. The angry, frightened crowd was past minding its manners, and at times the rush for the doors was carried on almost with savagery; women were buffeted— and buffeted back—and children swept away in the press. William and his friend—she was the sturdier as well as the taller of the two—clambered up the steps of a covered truck and were thrust through its opening by the weight of those pressing behind them. The truck, when they gained it, was close, evil-smelling and crowded; so crowded that many had to keep their feet for lack of the floor space to sit. When the struggle for places was over— and it was not over quickly—the train was packed end to end with sweating and exhausted travellers.

There followed a journey that to those who endured it seemed endless, a crawl punctuated with halts. The halts were lengthy as well as frequent; sometimes in sidings where refugees perforce gave place to troop trains, sometimes in junctions where they pulled up indefinitely at a platform and where worn-out officials could give no information as to when a fresh start would be made. The waits, wearisome as they were, were by far more endurable than the wretched stages in between; which were stages of sweating heat and smells, of stifling and cramped discomfort. On the platform, at least, it was possible to stretch and breathe; in the vans it was aching backs and bones and a foulness that thickened with the miles. Children wept and sickened as the hours crawled by and all through the darkness their crying was never stilled; as wretched little wailing or angry howl, it mingled always with the throb and clank of the train.

The delicate chill of morning was as nectar after the stench of the crowded night. By special mercy, just as dawn broke they drew up in a siding with fields to the right and left of them; neither William nor his friend was asleep when the train stopped, and, crawling over recumbent bodies on the floor of the van, they dropped down stiffly from their pen and stood breathing in the clean, cool wind. With their damp clothes sticking to their heated bodies, they sucked the air into their lungs—even William, blind with his misery, conscious of the calm loveliness of morning on stretches of green after the reek of the lantern-lit van. His companion, shuddering at the sight of her hands, went in search of water and discovered a tap on the platform; whereat William, in his turn, drank thirstily and soused hands and face before they settled down in a field at the side of the line. There, on the good green turf, they shared the last remnants of their package of food, some bread and an apple apiece. for all the hours they had spent on the train they had accomplished only some half of the distance to Paris; and as refreshment rooms—closed or cleared out by the troops—could no longer be counted on to supply the needs of the traveller, they had little prospect of further sustenance till they reached their journey's end. They ate their small meal sitting as far as they deemed safe from the train and the crowd it had disgorged—ate it in silence, for William had not yet found speech. His world, for the time being, was formless and void, and, as such, incapable of expression.

All day they travelled, as they had travelled on the day before: in jolted crowds, in squalor, in heat, to the sound of the misery of children. They ached, they wearied, they sweated, they thirsted—they halted and lurched on again; too wearied even for impatience, they endured without complaint until even the children were past crying. The sun was low on the horizon when William, drowsily stupid, raised his head from his knees as his friend touched him on the arm. He looked up stupidly—the train was plodding through forest; he had ceased to hope for the journey's end and sat for the most part with his head on his knees in a dull, half-dozing resignation.

"If we don't stop again," she told him, "we ought to be in fairly soon. I think that's Chantilly we've run through. We're only half an hour from Paris—in ordinary times, that's to say."

The times were not ordinary and they took more than half an hour—very much more—to get over the twenty odd miles. They slowed to a crawl for the last stretch of the journey, and outside Paris, between Paris and St. Denis, they halted and waited till well after night had fallen. But at long last the interminable wait was ended and they creaked and crept forward to a platform of the Gare du Nord—where William for the first time set foot in the capital of France. As he did so he remembered a fact that had hitherto slipped his memory—that Heinz and his companions, when they took his pocket-book, had left him without a penny. So far the loss of his purse had not troubled him; he had lived as the beasts live and been cared for even as they; but Paris was civilization where money would be needed for a lodging. He had no resource but his companion, and, as they drifted along with the slow-moving mass on the platform, he appealed perforce to her.

"I'm afraid," he stammered, "I've got no money. They took it away from me—the Germans."

She reassured him briskly with: "Don't worry about that—I've got plenty. I'll settle the hotel and the journey—you can pay me when we get back to London. Stick close to me, whatever you do; if I once lose you in this crowd I shall never find you again."

He replied with a mutter of thanks, and, obeying her injunction to stick close, was crushed, in her wake, past the barrier at the end of the platform, past the heated officials who were striving to deal with the needs of the influx of refugees, and finally out of the station. There, in the open space before the Gare du Nord, he stepped back suddenly from the world of nightmare into the world as he had always known it. The wide, lit street in front of the station was filled with a moving and everyday crowd, in his ears were the buzz of the taxi and the warning clang of the tram. The change from the horrible to normal surroundings—from brutality and foulness to the order of a great town—was so sudden and complete that it took away his breath like a swift plunge into cold water; and as the life of the city enwrapped him and claimed him for its own, for one crazy moment it seemed to him that the last few days were impossible. Their fantastic cruelty was something that could not have been ... and he almost looked round for Griselda.

CHAPTER XIV

Edith Haynes knew her way about Paris; and the little hotel in a quiet side-street, where a taxi deposited herself and her companion, was one that had sheltered her in days less eventful and strenuous, and where Madame, in consequence, was compassionate and not contemptuous at being asked to shelter two late arrivals in the last stage of dirt and untidiness. William, before he sat down to eat, had exchanged his torn garments for the suit of an absent son, called up on the first day of mobilization; and for all his ache and dull stupor of sorrow, he knew something of the blessing of bodily relief when he washed in hot water and was clean. He had had no real sleep since the night before Griselda died; now the need for it came down on him like a heavy cloud and, great as was also his need for food, he could hardly keep his eyes open through supper. When he woke next morning it was nearing midday and he had more than slept the clock round.

He pressed the bell as he had been told to do when he woke; and with the coffee and rolls that arrived at the summons came a pencilled note from his mentor. She had gone out to look up her relatives, and also to inquire about the time and manner of the journey from Paris to London; she wrote that she might not be back at the hotel for some hours, but the envelope that enclosed her communication enclosed likewise a tactfully proffered loan for the immediate needs of her fellow-traveller's wardrobe. But for the reminder it would have hardly occurred to him that his wardrobe was in need of renewal; he had grown so accustomed in the last long days to being ordered, guided, or driven that he had lost the habit of directing his own doings. As it was, he breakfasted, dressed himself again in the suit of Madame's absent son, and was instructed by Madame herself where to find a barber for an overdue shave and an outfitter capable of English. Thither he went, made his purchases mechanically and returned to the hotel with his new suit of black in a parcel. It seemed to him, as he walked the Paris streets, as he bought and paid and spoke of things that did not matter, that his sense of loss and his longing for Griselda was stronger even than in the first hours after her death. It was accentuated by his contact with the civilized, the normal; by the sights and sounds of the everyday world to which Griselda belonged. She had had no place in the strange French village where she died, no place in the misery and dirt of the crowded truck;

but here where life, to all seeming, was as usual, where the streets were like enough to English streets to produce, after country solitude and the savagery of bloodshed, the illusion of dear familiarity: here she should have walked with her arm in his. Here she would have chatted, have gazed in shop windows and bargained ... and long years faced him with their deadly never as he went his way without her.

Later, when he had returned to the hotel and changed into his new black suit, a wild fit of useless rage came over him—and alone in his third-floor bedroom he cursed the devils who had killed his wife, the devils who had made the war. Under his breath, lest he should be heard in the corridor, he called down the vengeance of God on their evil heads, breaking inevitably, as his own store of invective gave out into lyrical reminiscence of that Biblical lore with which his mother had imbued him through Sunday after Sunday of his childhood; believing in the God whose existence he had usually ignored (and often doubted) because of his need of an avenger and a present help in his trouble. In that moment the God whom he sought—and it may be found—was the Lord God of Hosts, the Mighty One of Israel, Who was wont to strike the wicked and spare not; and the desire of his shaken and rebellious soul was even as the desire of him who sang out his hatred by the alien waters of Babylon. The hotel chambermaid put an end to his whispered prayer and anathema by tapping on the door to inform him that lunch was waiting on the table.

Edith Haynes, when she returned in the late afternoon with news that the journey could be made on the following day by way of Dieppe and Folkestone, found him clad in his new-bought mourning for Griselda and poring over English newspapers. His eyes were still haggard and moved her to pity, but she took it as a good sign that his stupor of grief had passed and that he had begun (as his first question told her) to feel a need for more information which might bridge the month's gap in his knowledge of the outer world. She gave him, with such detail as she had in her possession, the story of the outbreak of war and the causes thereof: and from her he learned for the first time of the ultimatum to Servia, and the tension thereby created; of the political consequences of the invasion of Belgium, and the feverish days of hesitation in England that had ended, on the Fourth of August, with the formal declaration of war. He listened, sometimes puzzled but always intent, from time to time putting a question that revealed his blank ignorance of the network of European politics; to which she replied as clearly as she could, showing him maps and talking on in the hope of distracting him from the thoughts behind his haggard eyes. By degrees she gleaned, from his hesitating queries and disconnected comments, some understanding not only of his profound ignorance of the forces that had brought about the war, but of the upheaval of his mind and soul which was the direct and inevitable consequence of the loss of his former faith. Once or twice as they talked he quoted her scraps and jerks of anti-militarist propaganda—from Faraday, from orators of the Trades Union Congress, from a speech of Philip Snowden's in Parliament urging the reduction of the Navy—and she saw that he was trying to justify to himself his attitude and creed of yesterday. In the midst of a quotation from Faraday on the general strike as a certain preventive of war, he broke off suddenly to appeal to her with: "Every one thought he was right. He seemed so sure. I didn't see how he could be wrong!"

She noticed that, wherever their talk might stray, he came back, time and again, to his central fact—that the blankly impossible had happened and the jest was a brutal truth. That, in the beginning, was all his mind had laid hold of; now, the first stage of amazement over, he was groping instinctively, and perhaps unconsciously, after rights and wrongs of quarrel, and striving to understand how the impossible had come into existence. Edith Haynes had not passed her life in the atmosphere of Internationalism, and would have been more than human had she been an impartial guide to him where the causes of war were concerned—just as he would have been more than human had he been capable of impartial guidance. What he lacked in patriotism he made up in personal suffering; he hated the German because he had been robbed of his wife, and it added but little to the fire of his hatred to learn of faith broken with Belgium. If he listened intently when she told of it, if he pored over newspaper paragraphs dealing with German cruelty to the conquered, it was because they fitted with his mood and justified the loathing in his soul.

It was his persistent poring over English newspapers that brought him in the end the salvation of a definite purpose. An article in *The Daily Chronicle*— some days old—described the beginning of the recruiting campaign for the raising of Kitchener's Army; he read it as he read everything else that explained or described the war. At first the article was nothing but news to him, a mere statement of facts; but as he read further a meaning flamed into the news. Bereft as he was of guidance, his mind swinging rudderless in chaos, he was waiting unconsciously for the man or the impulse that could seize on his helpless emotion and give purpose and direction to his life; thus the journalist's vigorous appeal to the nation's patriotism was driven home by the force of his own experience and became an appeal to himself. The writer had illustrated his argument in the obvious manner, by reference to the condition of invaded Belgium and the suffering of her people under the hand and heel of the enemy; he wrote of women outraged, of hostages killed, of cities laid waste, and of houses fired with intention. He was spurred by indignation, by pity and a natural patriotism, and had laid on his colours—to all but William—with a vivid and forcible pen. To William, as he read, the result seemed lame and pitiful, an inadequate babbling of the living horrors that had burned themselves into his soul; but for all its weakness—perhaps because of it—the article gave him the impulse for which he had been waiting in torment. It may have been his very sense of the inadequacy with which it described what he had known that set his imagination to work, that drove home its purport and made of it a lead to his blind and whirling emotions. He read and re-read while he quivered with impatience at its failure; if the man had seen what he had seen, if the man had lost what he had lost, he could not have argued so tamely. His pen would have been dipped in fire; he would have written so that all men reading him would have rushed to arms. The paper dropped from his hands to the table and he sat staring at a picture of his own making—of a crowd bitter and determined, moved by the tale of wrongdoing to a righteous and terrible wrath. He saw it setting forth to execute justice and avenge innocent blood ... and himself one of it, spurring and urging it on. So he first visualized himself as a soldier—an unscientific combatant of the Homeric pattern, but nevertheless a soldier. The vision thrilled and inspired him, and out of the deep waters of his impotent misery he clutched at the knowledge that he could act, resent, resist; that, ceasing to suffer as the slave suffers, he could give back blow for blow.

There was enough of the old leaven in him to bring him up suddenly, and with something like a round turn, as he realized that the act of striking blow for blow against the German would involve the further act of enlistment and the wearing of the King's uniform. His first mental vision of his warrior crowd had been vague as well as Homeric; he had only seen faces uplifted by courage, not the khaki and buttons below them—seeing himself rather as an avenger of Griselda than as a soldier of the British Empire. But it was only for a moment that he shied Like a nervous horse at the bogey of the "hired assassin." The prophets from whom he had learned his one-time contempt for the soldier were no longer prophets to him, and his conversion was the more thorough from his ingrained and extremist conviction that the opposite of wrong must be right. Conversion, in the sense in which the word is employed by the religious, describes most clearly the process through which he had passed: conviction of ignorance, the burden of Christian; a sense of blind longing and humiliated confusion—and now, at the end, light flashed on him suddenly, salvation figured by the sword.... It was, so to speak, but a partial salvation. He had lost his capacity for absolute faith, for the rapture that comes of infallibility; but he was of all men the last who could live without guidance, and his new creed had at least this merit—it was supported by his own experience. Its articles, had he formulated them, would have been negative rather than assertive—I have ceased to believe in the old, rather than I believe in the new; but it gave him that working hypothesis without which Life to him was impossible.

When he took his seat, next morning, in the train bound for Dieppe, his mind was made up—made up fiercely and definitely—on his future course of action; and as a result something that was by comparison peace had succeeded to the chaos and dazed rebellion of his first few hours of loss. His companion noticed the change in his manner and bearing; it was not that he seemed more resigned, but that he had ceased to drift—his eyes were as haggard as yesterday, but not so vague and purposeless. So far during their brief but close acquaintance she had treated him perforce as she would have treated a child—providing for his bodily and mental needs and giving him kindly orders; now, ignorant and obedient as he still was in the matter of foreign travel, he was once more a reasonable being. He was still for the most part sunk in his own thoughts, but not helplessly and endlessly so; he was capable of being roused and at intervals he roused himself. Once when they halted she was struck by the intentness with which he gazed at a trainload of soldiers in khaki—new come from England and moving up from Havre to the front. They crossed at a wayside station, and the two trains stood side by side for some minutes while William craned out of the window to stare at the brown young faces that were thrust from the opposite carriages. The sight moved him, if not in the same fashion as it moved his companion; he felt no tightening of the throat and no pride in the men themselves. What kept his head at the window till the train moved off was chiefly the thought that soon he would be even as these sunbrowned men of war, the personal desire to know what manner of men they were, how they lived and moved and had their daily military being. Hitherto a soldier of the home-grown variety had been to him nothing more definite than an impression of uniform, khaki and occasionally red; now, with the eyes of his newborn interest, he became aware of detail that had formerly escaped him, and compared him in figure, in face and garment, with Heinz and Heinz's companions. These hot-faced lads smoking pipes and calling jests would be his own comrades in days to come; thus he studied their features, their dress, their manner, as a small boy scans and studies the bearing of his future schoolfellows. If he did not thrill at the sight of young men about to die, he sent with them (remembering Griselda) his strong desire for their great and terrible victory.

Those were the days just before Mons was fought, when France (and others with her) was hopeful of a war that would end at her frontier and beyond it; when, whatever her wiser soldiers may have known, her people in general had no premonition of the coming retreat of the Allied Armies and the coming peril of the capital. There were still some ignorant and optimistic days to live before France as a whole would be stunned by the curt official admission that the enemy was well within her borders—since his battle-line stretched across the country from the Vosges mountains to the Somme. As for railway communication on the western lines, the rush of returning tourists that had followed on the outbreak of war was over, and the rush from Paris that began with the new threat of Kluck's advance was as yet a thing of the future. Thus William and his companion, though they travelled slowly and with lengthy halts, travelled in comparative comfort—finding in unpunctuality and a measure of overcrowding but little to grumble at after their journey by cattle-truck to Paris.

Rouen kept them waiting an hour or two, and there was another long, purposeless halt on the boat in Dieppe Harbour; so that it was nigh upon sundown when they slipped into the Channel and headed north-westward for Folkestone. The day, very calm with the stillness of perfect summer, was even as that day but a month ago when William and his little bride had steamed away from Dover, sitting deck-chair to deck-chair, touching hands when they thought no one saw them. And remembering the fading of those other white cliffs, William's heart cried out against God.

It was well past midnight when they slid into Folkestone Harbour where again there were long delays; so long that morning was red over France when the train drew away from the pier. It was during the two-hour journey to Charing Cross that William first spoke to his friend of his purpose of becoming a soldier; they were not by themselves in the carriage, but the other occupants nodded off to sleep soon after the train had left Folkestone, and for all practical purposes he and Edith Haynes were alone. She was surprised by the announcement, more surprised perhaps than she should have been—less on account of his previous record than because his appearance and manner were so utterly unmilitary. The British soldier of pre-war days was a type, a man of a class apart; it was a type and class to which William Tully was far from approximating, and she found it impossible to picture his essentially civilian countenance between a khaki collar and cap. Her surprise must have shown in her manner, for he began to explain in jerks.

"It seems the only thing to do," he said. "You can't sit down and let it go on; when you've seen what I've seen, you've got to do what you can. And they want men—they're asking for them. The papers say they want all the men they can get ... it's got to be stopped—that devilry—somehow or another ... and there doesn't seem any other way..."

His voice tailed off and he turned his eyes away—to the flying fields where the dew was still wet and the shadows still long upon the grass. When, a few minutes later, he told her suddenly, "It was just as pretty as this—where it happened," she knew that he was mentally transforming the peace and greenery of a Kentish landscape into the background of such an imitation of hell as he had lived through in the Forest of Arden.

It was not till they were well on the London side of Tonbridge that he turned again to his companion. Something that she had said in appreciation of his decision—a kindly meant phrase that commended his courage—had seemingly been held in his mind.

"I don't want you to think it's courage, and I don't want you to think I'm making any sacrifice—I'm not. I'm enlisting because I want to enlist— and there isn't anything else for me to do. Everything's gone now—I haven't anything to go back to. No duties or ... I don't see how you can call it a sacrifice."

He swallowed and halted again and she could only nod in silence. She knew enough of him by this time to know that what he said was truth, having learned in the course of their days of acquaintanceship that he had lost even more than his newly made wife, his hopes of a home and children. In very deed he had nothing to go back to, neither home nor daily occupation; in losing his cocksure, infallible creed he had lost the interests wherewith his days had been filled. His meetings, his busy committees, the whole paraphernalia of his agitator's life, were with yesterday's seven thousand years. Even if Griselda had not died he, knowing what he knew, would have had to begin life again.

Near Chislehurst, reminded of the nearness of London, he put an apologetic question.

"You'll think me very ignorant," he said, "but you see I've never had anything to do with soldiers. Have you any idea how you set about joining the Army?"

She explained that he had only to offer himself, and turned up an English newspaper bought the day before at Dieppe to point out a paragraph giving the situation of the various London recruiting stations. He studied it with interest and showed her that the nearest to Charing Cross was a station on the Horse Guards Parade. She had not understood that his intention was to enlist at the moment of arrival in London, and suggested a delay of a day or two for rest if not for reflection: the life before him was a hard one physically, and he had been passing through a week of exhaustion both physical and mental. To her arguments he shook his head, stubbornly impatient; he was so urgent to translate his new convictions into immediate action that it was with difficulty she prevailed on him to delay at Charing Cross for breakfast, and only manoeuvred him into the hotel by assuring him—whether rightly or wrongly she knew not—that it was as yet far too early in the day for any recruiting official to be at his post. On that assurance he yielded, and they took their last meal together.

She had contracted an odd species of affection for the little bereft and destitute man whom chance had thrown on her hands in his hour of need; it was difficult for her to rid herself of a sense of responsibility for him and his doings: and as they disposed of their eggs and bacon she found herself wondering, with tears in her throat, how he could come through the discipline and hardship for which his soft life had done so little to prepare him. It was pathetic and even ridiculous to think of him as a soldier, this wisp of a town-bred talker; to think of him marching and bearing arms in defence of such as herself—who topped him by a good two inches and had treated him almost as a child. She coaxed him to eat a good breakfast, dawdling over her own that he should sit and rest the longer; and when he suddenly remembered to ask her how much he owed her for the expenses of the last few days, she gave him, with the hastily invented amount, her address in Somerset and made him promise to write and keep her informed of his doings. He, on his part, shrinking instinctively from those who had shared his errors in the old life, clung to her as the one person who understood the new world into which he had so lately entered—understood it because she was part of it; thus neither was unmoved when they shook hands as friends and parted at the door of the hotel. She entered a taxi for Paddington and he turned his face to Whitehall and the tent on the Horse Guards Parade.

As he walked down Whitehall his heart thudded loudly on his ribs. He remembered, with a sudden tremor of rage, how Heinz had boasted of his Kaiser at Westminster and a German entry into London. The very thought made London dearer and finer to him, and he had a vision of himself driving Heinz before him—Heinz and that other, the round-faced young man with black eyebrows who had worked his will on Griselda. He saw himself striking and stabbing at the round-faced young man—beating him down while he prayed in terror for a mercy that was not granted. His lips were a hard white line and his fingers clenched and unclenched. London! by God, it should be not London but Berlin!

He had never dreamed of rejection; he knew vaguely that recruits were required to pass some sort of medical examination, but the idea that his proffered services might be refused had never entered his head. Edith Haynes, like himself, had seen few English newspapers for weeks; thus he did not know till he came to enlist that the standard of measurement for recruits had been raised since the outbreak of war, and that he, standing under five foot five, was not up to the Army's requirements in the matter of breadth and inches. The knowledge took him like a blow between the eyes, and he stood with dropped jaw, incredulous—it was inhuman, it was monstrous that they should take from him his right to strike back. For a moment he had no words; he dressed mechanically, stupid with the shock— while the round-faced man grinned damnably over Griselda dead by the roadside.... And when, in the end, his speech came back and he tried to stammer an appeal, some one patted him good-naturedly on the shoulder, put his hat into his hand, and turned him loose into a world that had no meaning for him.

CHAPTER XV

There were many parallels to the case and conversion of William Tully in the first few weeks of the war. There is, and always will be, the self-centred temperament that can shut its eyes to the fact and tread the pathways of the paradise of fools, even if it treads them alone; but on the whole humanity is reasonable and, given a fact, however surprising and savagely unpleasant, accepts it because it must.

Those who struggled hardest against the acceptance of the War-Fact of 1914 were, naturally enough, those who had fiery little battles of their own to fight, and whose own warfare was suddenly rendered null and incompetent by a sudden diversion of energy and interest in the face of the national danger. The war was the successful rival of their own, their sectional strife, overshadowing its importance and sucking the life from its veins. Hence instinctively they sneered at it and strove to ignore its existence; hating it as a minor and incompetent artist may hate the greater professional rival who sings or acts him off the stage. Only by some such reasoning can one account for the fact that the aggressive and essentially militarist type of political enthusiast so often runs to pacifism where the quarrels of others are concerned.

But for the bitter mischance of a honeymoon spent in the Forest of Arden and the consequences thereby brought about, such would, very certainly, have been the mental attitude of William Tully in the August of 1914. His own battles would have absorbed his aggressive instincts, and, never having seen a shot fired in anger, he would have continued, for quite a long time, to think of other battles as enlarged street riots which were thoroughly enjoyed by the bloodthirsty soldiery who provoked them. He would have pooh-poohed the possibility of a war until the war actually broke out; and then, insisting that it was avoidable and should not have been, have clung angrily to his customary interests and done his small energetic best to keep his comrades from straying into that wider and bloodier field where they and their services would be lost to the sectional conflict. Such, very certainly, would have been his course of action had he made his wedding journey to Torquay. Fate and not temperament had willed it that he should be driven to enlist under the rival banner of nationality; but there were others of his kidney whom fate had not driven so brutally, and who, unable to effect, as William had done, a rapid transfer of allegiance and antagonisms, struggled desperately to uphold, in despite of war, their partially deserted standard. Of such was Faraday, dogged and fiercely indefatigable; though the man had soul and brain enough to feel the ground rock beneath him. His ignorance of European politics was a thought less profound than William's, but sufficiently profound to have bred in him a complete disbelief in the possibility of European war; hence his surprise at the international earthquake was almost as great as that of his former disciple. When the unbelievable happened he, as was but natural, was angry—all men are angry when the habit of years is interfered with; and in the first flush of his annoyance ascribed the falsification of his every prediction not to his own blundering, but to the sins of those who did not think as he did. Those who prophesied war—so he argued—had prophesied what they desired.... All the same, he was not, like William, devoid of the imaginative faculty; but the war was as yet a great way off and his hatred of the Government of his own country was real. With time he, too, came to understand that a people may have other foes than those of its own household and be threatened with death from without; when he was called up under the Conscription Act he went without protest, made an excellent soldier and died fighting in a night raid near Hulluch; but in the beginning the habit and association of years was too strong for him and his bitter dislike of his neighbour overpowered his fear of the German. During the first few weeks of the war he held peace meetings at considerable personal risk, which, as became a good fighter, he took, even with enjoyment; distributed printed appeals to pacifist and anti-British sentiment and wrote passionately, if with less than his usual clarity, in *The Torch*. He could not in honesty bring himself to defend every action of his country's enemies and was conscious of occasional difficulty and a sense of thin ice underneath him; at the same time it was against his tradition and principles to admit that the statesmanship of the land he was born in could ever have right on its side. Tradition and principles might have won hands down, making him ardently and happily pro-German, had it not been for the complication introduced by the attitude of other nations which, foreign even as Germany was foreign, had chosen to range themselves with England. Hence a difficulty in indiscriminate condemnation and a momentary confusion of thought and outlook of which Faraday himself was quite clear-brained enough to be conscious; it irritated him and he was sensible of failure and uncertainty.

On the day that William arrived in London and was refused for the British Army, Faraday held a small meeting in a hall in a Bloomsbury side street. The object of the meeting was to consider suitable methods of influencing for the better the existing and lamentable condition of popular opinion; the gathering was not open to the general public, only the initiated being present. Some thirty to forty of the initiated, chiefly secretaries, chairmen and other branch officials of the advanced socialist group of which Faraday was leading light and president—for the most part men, but with a sprinkling of women among them. They had been summoned together by letter and word of mouth; the meeting was private and consultative, described as for sympathizers only, and held at the headquarters of the Central London Branch—a large room, sparsely furnished with chairs and a platform, in the neighbourhood of Tottenham Court Road. One of the more muscular members of the branch kept watch and ward in the passage outside the hall, scrutinizing the comrades as they neared the door, lest any uninitiated person or disturber of peace should attempt to gain entry with the faithful; he was thrilled with a vague and grandiose conviction that the meeting was of perilous importance, passed in his familiars—they were all his familiars—with a mysterious nod and compared himself to a sentinel on duty in a post of extreme danger. He was a young man domiciled in the Hampstead Garden Suburb, with uncut hair, a flowing tie and a latent, if hitherto undeveloped sense of humour; and a year or two later, when the Army had claimed him, and he stood in the Ypres salient, in a post of extreme danger, he grinned unhappily between the shell-bursts as the night of the meeting came back to him.

Among his thirty or forty familiars he passed in William Tully—who had come to the hall mechanically, scarce knowing where his steps were guiding him. No wind of the meeting had come to him, but the place was one of his haunts—the Central London Branch, of which he was chairman, assembled there on business once a week. Further, it was used as the address of the Branch, and he was accustomed to call there almost daily for his official letters or the transaction of small official business. Thus it happened, at the close of a bewildered day, that he turned to it almost by instinct.

Perhaps it was a sense of homelessness that drove him to its open doors—for it was not until well towards evening that he had summoned up courage to enter his own dwelling, the little flat he had not yet lived in, made ready for himself and Griselda. If there had been anywhere else to go perhaps he never would have entered it; but his bachelor lodging, he knew, was let to a new tenant, and he had not money enough in his pocket to pay for a lodging elsewhere. His day had been spent on foot; after his refusal at the recruiting station he had walked he knew not whither—here, there, through street after street, that he might not stop and think; and when, in the late afternoon, he found himself sitting on the turf of Primrose Hill, he could not, for the life of him, remember the route by which he had reached it. Sheer weariness of body drove him to shelter, and half an hour later he was dragging his feet up the stairs that led to the flat.

The woman who was to "do" for himself and Griselda had been installed on the premises for some days past; since the outbreak of war she had been in hourly expectation of the arrival of her master and mistress and in some perturbation at the continued lack of news from them. As William was about to walk past the door she had opened to him she stayed him with an inquisitive question—he could not remember the form it took but knew that it must have referred to Griselda's absence, for he told her abruptly that his wife had died in France. She threw up her hands with a screaming exclamation as he hurried past her to shut himself into the bedroom.

There, afraid of her curious sympathy and questions, he shut and locked himself in; with the poignant loneliness of the brand-new furniture that he and Griselda had chosen and lovingly admired; with the poignant company of Griselda's photograph, smiling self-consciously from the centre of the mantelpiece and set in an ornate silver frame that was one of her wedding presents. He held it in his hands till the tears blinded him, kissed it sobbing and laid it face downwards.

The "general," burning with inquisitive sympathy, induced him, after one or two unsuccessful attempts, to open the door to her knocking; pressed on him, in spite of denials, a scratch meal of tea and poached eggs, and hovered round while he ate it. As befitted the occasion she held her apron to her eyes while she extracted as much as she could in the way of information. Later, as she washed up in the kitchen, she heard him moving from one tiny room to another—consumed with a restless misery and a restless wonder as to what he should do with his life. Still later she heard him go out again; though he had hidden away the self-conscious photograph, thrusting it out of sight into a drawer, the brand-new furniture was always there and always waiting for Griselda. The moment came when he could no longer suffer its company and went out into the street to avoid it. Other purpose in walking he had none—and thus it happened that, mechanically and without intent, he drifted into the Bloomsbury side-street where Faraday held his meeting.

The important doorkeeper would have greeted him with more than a nod—would gladly, in fact, have detained him after his four weeks' absence to exchange comments and views on the European situation; but William, in entering, made no response to his "Hallo, back again!" which it may be he did not even hear. He walked straight past the sentinel and into the bare familiar room—where everything, from the seats to their occupants, was just as it had been and where every face was known to him. Time, for a moment, turned back in its traces and yesterday unrolled before his eyes. He gazed at it and sat down slowly—by himself in the last row of chairs.... Edwardes, the Central London secretary, was hugging his ankle as he always hugged it, and Mrs. Jay-Blenkinsop, the formidable treasurer of the Golder's Green branch, frowned through her pince-nez at the speaker with her chin uplifted as of old, wore the same capacious sandals—her crossed knees showed them—and the same cold-gravy-coloured robe. And her son, young Jay-Blenkinsop, as his habit was, sprawled sideways on one chair and curled his long limbs round another. It was all as it had been; and Faraday, on the platform, was speaking with the accents of yesterday.

The important doorkeeper was not the only comrade who had noticed William's return: one or two heads were turned as he came in, but for the most part the audience was intent on the words of the speaker. The heads that turned made some sign of pleased recognition to which William responded automatically, unknowing that he did so. From his seat near the door his eyes wandered slowly over the platform, the hall and its occupants—slowly and with a dull and detached curiosity. What he saw there and heard was unreal, like a scene in an unconvincing play; he had a sense of looking at these people from a great way off, of hearing their voices from a distance. Something separated and held him removed from them.... He had great difficulty in giving his attention to what the speaker was saying; yet in the old days Faraday had always stirred him and to-night he was speaking well.

From thirty to forty convinced adherents assembled at a private conference are not the material upon which a public orator usually throws away his best endeavours; but Faraday that night was speaking not so much to his audience as to himself. Unadmitted, even to his secret soul, he had great and fierce need of conviction; it was with his own doubts that he wrestled, at his own head that he flung both his jeers and his arguments. He was of a finer because more intelligent mould than the Edwardeses and Jay-Blenkinsops who heard him and who were still thinking of the European tragedy as a red herring drawn by the cunning politician across the path of progress. Not for him was their happy imperviousness to the new idea, and, looking down from his platform on their assembled faces, it may have struck him, not pleasantly, that these people were in part of his making; they were, at any rate, the product of a system of which he, in common with politicians of every creed, had not scrupled to make full use.

Be that as it may, he spoke feelingly and well that night; far better and more feelingly than was needed by the numbers, the attitude and calibre of his audience, which was comfortably and stubbornly determined to agree with him before he opened his mouth. He had not come to the meeting with intent to be so lengthy and urgent; he had planned to be nothing more than brief and business-like, to give and invite suggestions for a vigorous prosecution of the anti-war campaign; but when he rose to open the discussion he was carried away by his own doubts and emotions; and the "few remarks" he had thought to make flared out into a veritable speech. He fought with and poured scorn on himself in the name of others, rallying his feebleness with argument and sneering at his own hesitations. Thus he spoke eloquently and deserved the applause which greeted him when he sat down.

Edwardes followed him, in response to the invitation for suggestions: a little be-spectacled Labour man whose ideal was a world of committees. There had been something alive about Faraday's outpouring; it was the speech of a man who, however resentfully, understood that the world had moved. But as Edwardes quacked earnestly about branch propaganda as an antidote to militarism and a means of diffusing the international idea, the sense of unreality descended again upon William. Branch propaganda— little leaflets and meetings—when guns made a pulp of flesh and blood, and men were being shot against walls! Resolutions in minute-books against wrongs like Griselda's and his own! For the first time for many days he felt a desire to laugh, and, if it had not been for his sense of the distant unreality of the proceedings, perhaps he would have been moved to actual expression of perverted and unmirthful mirth.

It was young Jay-Blenkinsop who made the proceedings real to him; and, but for his intervention at the end of the discussion, it is probable that William himself would have taken no part in it. He would have listened for a little, perhaps to the end, and then crept out to his loneliness; but Jay-Blenkinsop roused him and swept him out of himself ... Edwardes quacked earnestly for ten minutes or so: the aggrieved outpourings of a soul to which the really serious fact of the war was that it had caused a certain amount of backsliding and even desertion amongst the weaker brethren of his branch; and when he sat down, after a moment of silence, Jay-Blenkinsop rose to his feet. (In the dark ages that had ended a week ago William thought highly of Edgar Jay-Blenkinsop, esteeming him a youth of great promise.) With his hands in his pockets, his broad shoulders lolled against the wall and his hair, as usual, drooped over an eyebrow, he drawled out fine scorn upon the leaders of the Labour Party for their treachery to the cause of the People and their lack of the sense of Brotherhood. There was no particular purport in his vaguely scathing remarks, which (the meeting being nominally for business purposes) might well have been ruled out of order; but he was enjoying the sound of his own full voice and his mother gazed up at him admiringly.

It was more himself than his vague remarks that made William flare and see red—his six feet of conceited boyhood propped sprawlingly against the wall. As he listened he was gripped with a sudden hatred of Jay-Blenkinsop, a hatred that had its roots in envy of his physical perfections; it was for lack of that broad deep chest and those long strong limbs that the recruiting officer would have none of him ... and a muscular boy, a potential soldier, lolled hands in pockets and cracked ignorant jests at men who knew better than he did, at the agony of such as himself. As the young man drawled onward William breathed fast and thickly and clutched at the chair in front of him: till Jay-Blenkinsop, having sufficiently scarified the official representatives of Labour, went on to some smartly turned gibes at the recruiting campaign and the gulls who were caught by its appeals. One of his sarcasms brought him the ready laugh he had counted on—and something on which he had not counted; at the tail of the laugh came, imperative and raucous, the order, "Sit down, you young fool!"

Every head in the room went round with indignation to William—whom most of the gathering, Faraday included, now noticed for the first time. He was on his feet, stiffened and pallid with passion; but after the cry that had cut short Jay-Blenkinsop he stood silent, with his lips apart and his hands clutching at a chair-back. His fingers knotted and worked as they clutched and his mouth was twisted and quivering; he stood like an animal backed into a corner, defying the astounded eyes and the open incredulous mouths of those who had once been his comrades ... Most incredulous of all was the mouth of Mrs. Jay-Blenkinsop, who gaped in amazement at the unprovoked attack on her son.

"May I ask——?" began Edgar Jay-Blenkinsop, less slowly and languidly than usual—whereat William, hearing the silence broken, also found words to his tongue.

"You may ask," he interrupted, "oh yes, you may ask! Anything you like. But for God's sake don't lay down the law and make ignorant assertions— for God's sake don't do that. You mustn't lay down the law until you know something, until you've really tried to find out. Then, perhaps, you'll have a right to speak; now when I hear you, I—I——" From sheer sense of the inadequacy of words his voice tailed huskily away; then, with an odd little snarl at his auditors, he burst out savagely afresh: "You child, you great impudent jackanapes! You stand there and dare to make jokes about the hell that other men have burned in. The flames and the blood and the guns and people dying in the road. You talk blank foolery and laugh about it—you laugh and turn up your nose. You think you're clever—and enlightened— and it sickens me, sickens me to hear you!"

He finished on a note that was almost a scream, and they looked at him aghast and dumfoundered. It was his face that held them even more than his disconcerting words—all but Edgar Jay-Blenkinsop, who, pricked in his vanity, would have accepted the challenge and started again had not Faraday silenced him with a turn of the head and a gesture. Still more pricked in his vanity he slid to a chair, muttering sulkily and red to the neck.

"Tully——" began Faraday with reproof in his voice—but Tully defied even his mentor. Not savagely and with contempt, as he had defied and decried Jay-Blenkinsop, but as one who had a right to be heard.

"He mustn't talk like that till he knows something. It's child's talk— ridiculous babble. I know what I'm saying—I've come from it—and I've a right to tell him what I know. Not one of you here has seen what I have— you're just guessing. When a shell bursts ... I've seen a man with his legs like red jelly and a horse..." he choked at the memory. "That's being a soldier— let him fight and he'll find it out. Now he thinks it's what he said just now—a sort of game that they like. Everything he said was mean little nonsense— how dare you listen to it and laugh at his silly little jokes? What's the good of saying that it shouldn't happen? Of course it shouldn't happen—we all know that—of course it shouldn't happen, but it does. And you can't stop it with sneers about soldiers and Kitchener.... It's hell and the mouth of hell— I've seen it. He says he wouldn't lift a finger to keep them out. Do you know why he says that? It's because he can't imagine what it means. I would. I'd die to keep them out, because I've seen ... I've seen a man shot—not a soldier, just an ordinary man—put against a wall and shot while his wife howled like a dog. Two men—and their wives standing by. They might do that to him if they came—has he ever thought of that?—while his mother howled like a dog." He shot out a quivering finger at the open-mouthed Mrs. Jay-Blenkinsop. "And his women—would he let them do as they liked with his women? They would if they came here—he can take my word for it they would. Would he ask them in politely and shake hands and give them drinks and let them? ... If they came, people would run from them, leaving everything they had—beggars. Would he like to be driven and beaten and made to work like a slave? I've had that—I've been driven and beaten and made to work. And I've run from them and starved and hidden because I was afraid. And my wife died—they killed her——"

There was a gasp, a rustle of movement and a sudden straightening of backs. Every one in the room knew Griselda Tully, many quite intimately, and not a few had been at her wedding; amazement and wrath against the disturber of the peace gave way to a real consternation, and in the silence that followed the momentary rustle William heard Faraday's "Good God!" ... They stared at him in dumb consternation, dimly conscious, perhaps, that they were in the presence of an eternal fact, and that the little man who stabbed at them with a trembling forefinger was the embodiment of that sense of injustice and agony which makes men cry to Heaven for vengeance and, Heaven failing them, take the sword and smite for themselves. Dolly Murgatroyd, Griselda's bridesmaid, who had twice accompanied Griselda to Holloway, saw and shrank from the reality of that tortured revolt which for years she had striven to simulate under the lash of her leaders' bombast.... In face of the fact that was William their theories wilted and failed them, and the new black suit of their comrade Tully was to them as the writing on the wall at the feast of Belshazzar—and came, like that other writing on the wall, at the moment when the evil from which they had hidden their faces was an evil actually accomplished. In each man's heart was a faint reflection of the amaze that had fallen on William and Griselda when their world first crumbled about them.

The sudden movement, the chairman's exclamation and the abashed silence that followed it checked William and brought him to a standstill; speech failed him and he stood with his mouth half open while the meeting stared at him motionless. There was a blank period of tension, of awkward stillness hi the presence of emotion, and then Faraday coughed uncertainly and moved. Probably he intended to say something, perhaps to adjourn the meeting; but his movement and the breaking of silence with his cough gave William back his voice and he spoke before Faraday began.

"And they won't take me in the Army. Although my wife has been killed they won't take me in the Army. I'm not tall enough; I'm only five foot five, and they won't take me. I've seen my wife die—she died in the road—and they refused me when I tried to enlist. If I were only two inches taller—God in Heaven, if I were two inches taller!"

The high, tight voice broke suddenly and he wept with his face in his hands. For the space of a painful moment there was no sound in the room but his sobs—no man knowing what to do or where to turn his eyes until Faraday came down from the platform. The tread of his feet on the gangway broke the spell of embarrassed silence—and chairs were moved softly and the occupants looked away from William as Faraday took him very gently by the arm and led him out into the street.

CHAPTER XVI

There was to be a gulf henceforth between William and Faraday, and the twain who had once lived so near together were to see but little of each other; yet it was Faraday who gave him the first word of comfort as he walked by the side of his former disciple on the road to William's flat. "If," he said suddenly and awkwardly—they were nearing their destination and it was the first time he had opened his lips since he led William out of the hall—"if it's this recruiting business, this refusal, that's adding to your trouble, I don't think you need be too much discouraged. Honestly—you see it isn't necessarily final. I know for a fact they're refusing men now, because they can't equip them as fast as they come in. They haven't the uniforms, the accommodation, or the arms, and that's why they sent up the standard for recruits with a rush. But if the thing's as big as they say—the common talk is that Kitchener has prophesied three years of it, and it's very likely true—they'll be wanting every man who'll come in before they've done with it. Not only the big chaps—every one. It will merely be a question of a few months—at the outside only a few months. So I shouldn't take this refusal to heart."

His message of comfort cost Faraday something to deliver; it was the sheer wretchedness of the broken little man beside him that moved him to deny his principles, by implication if not in so many words. The only audible reply that he received was a sniff, but even in the darkness he knew that his inconsistency had not been wasted, and that William had gained from it some measure of help and consolation. He said no more, and they parted with constraint on the pavement outside the flat—to tread through the future ahead of them their separate and several ways. Faraday did not go back to his meeting; he left it to break up or pursue as it would, while he walked the streets restlessly alone.

Between the uttering and fulfilment of Faraday's prophecy William's way, for the next few weeks, was the way of drift and uncertainty; it was also the way of great loneliness, an experience entirely new to him. Loneliness not only by reason of the loss of his wife, but because of the gap that the war had made between himself and his former associates. With the ending of his platform and committee career he was cut off, automatically and completely, from the fellowship of those who had been his co-workers in the various causes and enthusiasms he had once espoused and advocated. It was not that all of his former co-workers would have disagreed with his altered point of view; his was not the only perversion to militarism the stalwarts had to deplore; it was merely that he ceased to meet them. All the same the new isolation in which he lived was largely due to his own initiative or lack of it, since many, even among the stalwarts would have given him kindly welcome and done their best to be of help to him personally; but after the meeting in Bloomsbury he felt small desire to seek them out. On the contrary, he shrank into himself and avoided, as far as possible, any contact with those whose very presence would remind him of the busy, self-satisfied life he had passed in their company, of the vanished, theoretical world where he had met Griselda and loved her. It was a real misfortune that his small private income, though to a certain extent affected by the war, was yet sufficient to keep a roof over his head and supply him with decent necessaries of food and clothing. Thus, he was not driven to the daily work of hand or brain that might have acted as a tonic to the lethargic hopelessness of his mood. Nature had not made him versatile and he had lived in a groove for years; and, his occupation as a public speaker gone, he was left without interest as well as without employment. More than once, goaded into spasmodic activity by some newspaper paragraph, he offered himself vaguely for war-work—only to be discouraged afresh by the offer of an entirely unsuitable job or by delays and evasions which might have discouraged men more competent and energetic than himself.

In one respect fortune was kind to him; he was able, within a week or two of his return to London, to get rid of the lease of the haunted little flat in Bloomsbury. The place was dreadful to him, with its empty demand for Griselda, and he left it thankfully for a lodging in Camden Town. There for some weeks he lived drearily in two small rooms, with no occupation to fill up the void in his life, passing hermit days in the company of newspapers and poring over cheap war literature; he bought many newspapers and much war literature and aroused the sympathy of his elderly landlady by his helplessness and continual loneliness. What kept him alive mentally was his thirsty interest in the war; anything and everything that dealt with it was grist to his mill, and he acquired necessarily in the course of his eager reading some smattering of European history and the outlines of European geography. The pamphlet and journal soon ceased to satisfy, and he felt the need of supplementing their superficial comments and sketchy allusions by reading that was not up-to-date. A newspaper denunciation of the Silesian policy of Frederick the Great led him to Macaulay and others on the Kaiser's ancestor, and references to the Franco-German War resulted in the borrowing from the nearest Free Library of a volume of modern French history. One volume led on to others and the local librarian came to know him as a regular client.

His reading was haphazard, but perhaps, for that reason, all the more informative and illuminating. So far he had acquired such small learning as he possessed on a definite and narrow plan, assimilating only such facts as squared with his theories and rejecting all the others; where his new studies were concerned the very blankness of his ignorance was a guarantee of freedom from prejudice. He stumbled amongst facts and opinions, making little of them and yet making much—since for the first time in his life there was no glib mentor to guide him and he was thrown on his own resources. With his theories demolished and his mind blank as a child's, he became aware of phases of human idea and striving of which he had known nothing in the past, and the resulting comprehension of the existence of spheres outside his own increased his sense of the impossibility of his previous classification of mankind into the well-intentioned and the evil. His own experience had shown him that there might be at least a third class—the ignorant, the mistaken, to which he, William Tully, belonged—and his reading, by its very vagueness, confirmed that personal experience. As he floundered through histories, bewildered and at random, he realized dizzily, but none the less surely, something of the vast and terrifying complexity of these human problems upon which he had once pronounced himself with the certainty of absolute ignorance.

The Free Library, though he knew it not, was a salve to his wounded heart; all unconsciously he had done the best for himself in applying his mind to matters of which his little wife had known nothing. Bismarckian policy and the Napoleonic Wars were topics he had not discussed and interests he had not shared with her; hence they tended to come between him and her memory and distract him from lonely brooding. Without his new studies he might have drifted into sheer melancholia and helplessness; as it was, he burned midnight gas over his books and kept his brain alive. In a measure his interest in his new studies was personal; the craving to strike back was always with him and his reading fed and fanned it; beginning without system he was naturally enough attracted by the drama and movement of the French Revolutionary and Napoleonic epoch, read avidly all that the librarian could give him on the subject and moulded his ideas of a soldier's life and military science on the doings of men of those days. The seed of hope that Faraday had implanted did not die, and he thought of himself as a soldier to be, while queer little ambitions flamed up in his barren heart. He read of Ney and Murat, who had carried marshals' batons in their knapsacks—until, the fervour of his obsession growing, he dreamed of himself as an avenging leader, and, with a half-confessed idea of fitting himself for the office, applied hours to the study of the art of war through the medium of an obsolete volume on military lore picked up from a second-hand bookstall in the Charing Cross Road. By its aid—it had been published in the early 'fifties—he attempted to work out the strategy of Kluck and Joffre, and spent long evenings poring over diagrams explanatory of the tactics of Napoleon at Montereau or the Archduke Charles at Essling.

For a time his only real human intercourse, and that by letter, was with Edith Haynes; he had written to her telling of his rejection for the Army and she wrote to him more than occasionally. She was fixed busily in her Somersetshire home, looking after the property of a brother fighting in Flanders, acting as bailiff and herself taking a hand in farm-work. For the first few weeks after Griselda's death she remained William's only friend in the new world of war, and it was not until he had been settled for nearly two months in his Camden Town lodging that he discovered that some at least of his former associates had seen fit, like himself, to reconsider their views and take up arms for their country. He ran against one of them—Watson, in the old days a fiery committee-member of his branch—in the garb of the London Scottish; and he did not know how lonely he had been until he spent an evening in the convert's company, talking his heart out, talking of the war and himself.

With the first announcement of the reduction in the standard of height for recruits he tried to enlist again and was again refused—this time by the doctor who seemingly had doubts about his heart. On the way home a fool woman, arrogating to herself the right to make men die for her, offered him a white feather as he stood waiting for his 'bus—whereupon he turned and swore at her using filthy words that were strange to his lips till her vapid little face grew scarlet. That day, for the first time, his books were no comfort to his soul and he thrust them away and sat brooding—understanding perhaps how personal and revengeful had been his interest in the lore of the past, understanding how strong had been the dreams and ambitions he had cherished in his empty heart. Watson, dropping in for a final chat before starting on foreign service, found him sullen and inert before his fire, and, casting about for a method of comfort, suggested application to another recruiting station; he knew, he said, of more than one man who, refused at a first medical examination, had been passed without trouble at a second. Hope was beaten out of William and he shook his head ... all the same, next morning he tubed to the other end of London, there to make his third attempt.

He asked his way to the townhall and in a species of dull resignation stood waiting his turn for the ordeal of medical inspection. When it came he went listlessly through the now familiar process, stripped, was weighed and measured, was pummelled, showed his teeth, answered questions. It was the stethoscope that had done the business yesterday, and would do it again to-day; not that there was anything the matter with him or his heart—it was just the blind cruel stupidity that was always and in everything against him.... While the doctor bent to listen he was wondering what he should do with to-morrow, what he should do with the next day, what he should do with his life!

He had made so sure of a third rejection that he could hardly believe his ears when he heard he was up to the physical standard required of a soldier of the King. "You've made a mistake," was on the tip of his tongue, and though he checked the words before they were uttered, he stood dazed and staring, much as he had done on the day he was first refused. He could not remember clearly what happened to him next or what he did; he went where he was told, he sat and waited, he repeated words which he knew must have been the oath; his fellows talked to him and he answered back ... but all he was conscious of was the stunning fact of his acceptance. It seemed to him Griselda must know and rejoice—and he had thoughts of her watching him, of her white soul blessing him to victory.

CHAPTER XVII

A pencilled scrawl despatched from a mushroom camp in the Home Counties told Edith Haynes that William was at last a soldier; it was brief, written shakily by a man tired in body but uplifted in spirit, informed her that he had just been absorbed into a London battalion, that he had not yet got his uniform, was sleeping in a barn and drilling hard and concluded with the words "Thank God!" She answered the scrawl by return of post and a few weeks later, hearing nothing, wrote again; but, in spite of her request for further news, for month after month she waited in vain for a successor to the shaky scribble.

When it came the war had been in progress a couple of years and the address was a procession of letters—whereof the three last were the B.E.F. that denoted service over-Channel. It was a restrained and correct little letter, on the face of it uninteresting and not much longer than the last, but differing from it in that it was written in ink and in the tidy, clerical hand which William had acquired in the days of his boyhood for the use of the insurance office. It expressed regret for his lengthy silence, but did not attempt to explain it; and went on to relate that before coming to France he had been an orderly-room clerk, that he was at present at an advanced base—he must not of course give its name—where he was employed in office work, principally the typewriting of letters. It concluded with an assurance that he had not forgotten her kindness and a hope she would write to him again ... and she read and re-read the polite little missive, half-guessing what lay between its lines.

It had been written in an interval of that typing of local official communications which was Private Tully's daily contribution to the waging of the European War; and it had not been written earlier because Private Tully was too sullen of heart to write.

For a few weeks only he had known what it was to be a soldier of England in the making; he had drilled, he had marched, he had learned to hold a rifle and his body had ached with the discipline. He had lain down at night so weary that he could not sleep, and he had risen giddily in the morning in fear of the day that was coming. Other men filled out and hardened with their training, grew healthy, muscular and brown—and he set his teeth and argued with himself that this stage of sick exhaustion was only a stage and in time he would be even as they. What he lacked in strength he made up in fiery willingness, overtaxing his energy by dogged efforts to keep level with broader shouldered, tighter muscled men, and steadfastly refusing to admit that his bodily misery was more than a passing discomfort. More than once a good-natured comrade suggested a visit to the doctor—whereat William would flush as at an insult and turn on the meddler almost savagely.

He held on longer than he could have done unaided, by virtue of much kindly help. Once, in a sudden need for sympathy he had told to one of his fellows the story of Griselda and his own conversion to militarism; and, unknown to himself, the story went the round of his mess. From the beginning the men had treated him with the instinctive kindness that the stronger feels for the weakling, but from that time forth their kindness was more than instinctive; they ranged themselves tacitly on the weakling's side in his struggle with his own deficiencies. Little odd jobs of cleaning and furbishing were done for him—often secretly, he knew not by whom—and no man was ever too weary to take on work that would spare him. They were in a conspiracy to save him from blunders—to warn him or shield him from consequences, and as far as camp life permitted they coddled him, with something of the sweet roughness wherewith Nelson was coddled by his captains.

All the same, and in spite of coddling, the breakdown came as it was bound to do in the end; the doctor who refused had been wiser than the man who passed him. There was nothing urgently or seriously wrong with his health; but he was not made soundly enough to stand the violent and sudden change from a sedentary life to a life of unceasing exertion. He had never taken much out-of-door exercise; had always trained or 'bussed it rather than travel afoot; and of late his days had been spent entirely between the four walls of his Camden Town sitting-room.

It was on the homeward stretch of a route march that his strength failed him suddenly and he knew that he could do no more; his pack was a mountain, his body was an ache, and a blackness closed upon his eyes. He fought very gallantly to save himself and, by the dogged effort of his will, kept going for a few minutes more. "I can do ten steps," he told himself and counted each step as he took it; then, the first ten accomplished, "Now I can do ten more." So he kept going for a few yards more and dragged foot after foot till he had reached the tale of two hundred; at which point—twenty tens—he staggered, fell out of the ranks in a faint and was brought back to camp on a stretcher.

That was the end of his soldiering with pack and rifle; from the day of his breakdown on the route march his platoon knew him no more and when he came out of hospital, some three weeks later, he was put on to clerical duties. As orderly-room clerk he handled a typewriter instead of a bayonet, and handled it steadily as the months lengthened into years. Others, his contemporaries, completed their training, left the camp, and went off to the front; he remained, at first savagely resentful and later sullenly resigned.

His conception of soldiering, derived as it was from his own brief and fiery experience in Belgium, from the descriptive articles of war correspondents and his reading of bygone campaigns, had never included the soldier who was merely a clerk. He had never realized that a man in uniform was not necessarily a man of blood; the revelation came to him only when he copied letters and routine orders, filed papers and, for all practical purposes, was back at his desk in the insurance office. His daily duties mocked and derided the hopes and ambitions wherewith he had joined the Army; and, ticking at his typewriter, he contrasted, half-ashamedly, the blank reality with the strenuous and highly coloured dream. One phase of that dream—inspiring then, ridiculous now—had shown him to himself as the hero of some bloody enterprise and the central figure of such a scene as he had read of in Napoleonic history; a scene of be-medalling and public praise in token of duty bravely done. He had pictured it often, awake and asleep ... and fancied Griselda looking down.

Slowly, under the benumbing influence of office routine, his revengeful ambitions faded, and with them his half-acknowledged hope of emulating Murat and Augereau. His interest in the war had been fundamentally a personal interest, and though there had grown up in him, by force of circumstance, a tardy consciousness of his Englishry, it was hardly strong enough to inspire him with pride in a humble and wearisome duty done in the name of England. Be it said in excuse for him that few men could feel pride in the labour of dealing with daily official communications—the duty of copying out vain repetitions and assisting in the waste of good paper. The stilted uselessness of half the documents was evident even to William; and there were moments when he told himself, in savage discontent, that he would have been less unprofitable in civilian idleness than busied in promoting futility.

For a time he was jolted out of his rut by his transfer to France in the August of 1916. He was drafted out, at a few hours' notice, with a batch of men destined for clerical duties, and found himself planted in a small French town round which camps were spreading in a fringe of tent and hutment, and where house after house was being rapidly annexed for the service of the British Army. But, save for change of scene and country, the new rut into which he had been jolted was twin to his old rut in England. It was the same clerk's life—this time in the office of a military department—but with longer and more irregular hours than fall to the lot of the ordinary civilian clerk, and with restrictions on personal freedom unknown since his days in the City. The Army kept him as tightly as his strait-laced mother; demanded as regular hours and refused, as steadfastly as she had done, to let him wander o' nights.

He filed, he copied, he ate his rations—and from the beaten track of his everyday life, the war seemed very far away. Sometimes in his off-hours, afternoon or evening, he would tramp up the hills that held the little town as in a cup to a point where, looking eastward, he could see the sudden flashes of the guns. The bright, fierce flashes in the evening sky were war, real war made visible and wickedly beautiful; such war as he had seen in the Ardennes village, and such as he had dreamed of fighting when he first donned his khaki tunic. And instead a chair and a typewriter in the Rue Ernest Dupont, the papers to be filed that a girl might have filed, the round of safe and disciplined monotony. That was war as he knew it: an office with flashes in the distance.

For a few days after his arrival in France his new surroundings interested him—the cobbled roads, the build of the houses, the sound of French in the streets; but once their strangeness had worn off he accepted and ceased to notice them. He was not sufficiently educated, sufficiently imaginative or observant, to take at anything beyond their face-value the various and incongruous types of humanity with which he was brought into contact. The strange life of Northern France affected him only where it touched him personally, and to him the sight of a turbaned brown trooper bargaining in the market-place with a swift-spoken, bare-headed Frenchwoman was an oddity and nothing more; just as the flamboyant façade of the great church of St. Nicholas was an oddity, a building unlike, in its mass and its detail of statuary, to the churches he knew of in London. He came across many such oddities—and having no meaning for him, they made but a passing impression. After a week or two he no longer turned his head at the sight of a gang of Annamite labourers or the passing of a detachment of heavy-booted German prisoners marched campwards at the end of their day; these things, like the ambulances crawling in a convoy from the station, like the shuttered French houses built squarely round courtyards, became part of the background of his daily life and he ceased to wonder or reflect on them. Perhaps his contact with alien races, with strange buildings and habits once unknown, may have increased his vague sense of the impossibility of fitting all men to one pattern, and of solving the problems of human misgovernment and government by means of the simple and sweeping expedients he had once been so glib in upholding; but on the whole it left him unaffected because little interested. His course of Free Library reading had placed him in possession of certain scattered facts concerning France, facts dealing chiefly with the First Napoleon and the German War of 1870; but for all the hot interest they had stirred in him once, they gave him small insight into the forces that had gone to the making of the country in which his life was spent wearily. He was lacking entirely in the historical sense, the sense that makes dead men alive; thus, in connection with the doings of present-day Frenchmen, his odds and ends of historical reading had little more meaning to him than the Late Gothic carving on the ornate portal of St. Nicholas.

The phase of warfare with which France familiarized him was not only secure and uneventful; as far as the native was concerned it was likewise prosperous. The town where he plodded through his daily toil was blessed as never before in the matter of trade and turnover; commercially it blossomed and bore good fruit in the deadly shade of the upas tree. The camps and the offices meant custom to its citizens, and, whatever the toll in the blood of its sons, it gained in its pocket by the war. The Germans, in 1914, had threatened but barely entered it; it had neither damage to repair nor extorted indemnity to recoup, and money flowed freely to the palms of its inhabitants from the pockets of the British soldier. Its neighbours, a few miles away, lay in hopeless ruin, their industries annihilated, their inhabitants scattered, their very outlines untraceable—beaten to death by that same chance of war which had spared the city in the cup of the hills and exalted her financial horn. Here were neither misery nor shell-holes; the local shopkeeper was solidly content, the local innkeeper banked cheerfully and often, the local farmer sold his produce to advantage and the volume of trade in the district expanded and burst new channels. Eating-houses broke out into English announcements concerning eggs, fried potatoes, and vegetables; English newspapers were plentiful as French in the shops and small boys cried them in the streets; and when the weekly market gathered in the shadow of St. Nicholas, to the stalls for hardware, fruit and cheap finery were added the stalls that did a roaring business in "souvenirs" for the English markets.

His days were steadfastly regular and steadfastly monotonous. Each morning by half-past eight he was seated in the office in the Rue Ernest Dupont; in a roomy house, most provincially French, built round a paved courtyard and entered from the street by an archway. A projecting board at the side of the archway bore the accumulation of letters which denoted the department by which the house had been annexed, and on the door of the room where William laboured was the legend "Letters and Enquiries."

At half-past twelve he knocked off for dinner and was his own master till three; then the office again till supper and after supper—with good luck till ten, with bad luck indefinite overtime. On Sundays he was his own master for the space of an afternoon, and now and again there were parades and now and again the "late pass" that entitled to an evening at liberty. When he first arrived he was fed and roofed in one of the camps on the borders of the little city; later, with half-a-dozen fellows, he slept and messed in the upper rooms of the building in which he did his daily work.... It was a life of bleak order and meticulous, safe regularity, poles apart from his civilian forecast of the doings of a man of war. There was small thrill of personal danger about its soldiering; the little city at the "Front" was far less exposed to the malice of enemies than London or the East Coast of England: and almost the only indication of possible peril was the occasional printed notice displayed in a citizen's window to the effect that within was a cellar "at the disposition of the public in case of alarm"—from aircraft. Once or twice during the first year that William dwelt there the anti-aircraft section grew clamorous on its hills and spat loudly at specks in the blue—which, after a few minutes, receded to the east while the city settled down without injury. The men in the town and quartered in the camps outside it were for the most part office-workers, men of the A.S.C., of Labour companies or Veterinary service; to whom the monotony of daily existence was a deadlier foe than the German.

His life had been unusually clean; partly, no doubt, from inclination to cleanliness, but partly through influence of circumstance. While his mother lived he had small opportunity for dissipation even of the mildest variety; and hard on her death had come the great new interests which his friendship with Faraday opened to him. Those interests had been so engrossing that he had little energy to spare from them; all his hopes and pleasures were bound up in his "causes," and the very violence of his political enthusiasms had saved him from physical temptation. Thus he had come to Griselda heart-whole and sound, and, even when his causes and his wife were lost, the habit of years still clung to him and the follies that came easily to others would have needed an effort in him.

Once or twice, in the soddenness of his discontent, he was tempted to turn to the gross pleasures of drink and worse in which others found distraction from their dullness; but the temptation was never an urgent one and there was no great merit in his resistance. One night he overdrank himself in a deliberate attempt at forgetfulness—whereupon he was violently sick, crawled to bed throbbing with headache, and did not repeat the experience.

He felt himself drifting mentally, and, to his credit, made efforts to save himself; tried to awaken an interest in the French language, bought a dictionary and phrase-book and attended bi-weekly classes in a neighbouring Y.M.C.A. hut. He spent a certain amount of his leisure in the Y.M.C.A. hut; borrowing books from its library, listening to its concerts, and now and again making one at a game of draughts. He made no real friends—probably because he was not in the mood for making any; with his comrades of the office he got on well enough, but there was no such tie between him and them as had existed between him and the men of his mess in the days when he first donned his uniform. The hope deferred that had sickened his heart had driven him in upon himself; then his desk-work was obviously well within his powers and outwardly there was nothing about him to call for special sympathy and kindliness. His fellows mostly looked on him as a harmless, uncompanionable chap who preferred to be left to himself.

By degrees William Tully was moulded to the narrow little life departmental and lived through its duties and hours of leisure taking not much thought for the morrow; in the Rue Ernest Dupont the war seemed much smaller, much farther away, than it had seemed at home in England, and, absorbed in its minor machinery, he could no longer consider it as a whole. The office and the daily details of the office, the companions he worked with, disliked and liked, loomed larger in his eyes than the crash of armies or the doings of men at the front. As a civilian he had wrestled with strategy and pored over maps; as a soldier of England he could not see the wood for the trees. And if he did not fall mentally to the level of that species of surgeon to whom war is an agency for the provision of interesting cases, it was merely because, unlike the surgeon, he had little enthusiasm for his work.

Inevitably, with the passing of month after month, the memory of Griselda grew less poignant; and with the soothing of his sense of loss there came about, also inevitably, a cooling of his fury for instant and personal revenge. He had not forgiven and would never forget, but he no longer agonized at his helplessness to strike a blow; in part, perhaps, because the discipline under which he lived had weakened his power of initiative. Though he chafed under discipline he learned to depend on it and became accustomed to the daily ordering of his life; and his early training in the insurance office stood him in good stead, so that he performed his duties with the necessary efficiency and smartness.... What remained with him, long after the memory of his dead wife had ceased to be an ever-present wound, was the sense of having been fooled by he knew not whom, of having been trapped and held by false pretences. The fact that his grievance was vague did not lessen its bitterness; it lay too deep for the grousing that he heard from others, and for the most he nursed it in silence, the silence of smouldering rebellion.

There were moments when his face must have been more communicative than his tongue; for one Sunday, an early spring Sunday as he sat on a hill above the town and stared vaguely at the skyline, a man addressed him with, "Are you feeling like that, mate?" and squatted on the grass beside him: a lean young man with a worn brown face—deeply lined on the forehead and with eyes, like a sailor's, accustomed to looking at distances.

"I'm like it myself," he went on without waiting for an answer, and stretched himself out on to his elbow. "These last few days it's been almost beyond holding in; it's the spring, I suppose, the good road weather and the sun. I don't mind it so much when there's mud and the country doesn't grin at you; I can stand it well enough then."

Lying stretched on his elbow he began to talk about himself. He was English-born and he had begun his career at a desk—staying there just long enough to save up his fare and a few pounds to start him in Canada. After that came a farm—to his thinking but a shade less narrow than the office; to be left for the rolling, the shifting life, the only life worth living. He had had his ups, he had had his downs—but always with his eyes on the distance. Ten fine years of it, American, African, Australian; the life independent where you shouldered your pack and gave men the go-by when you were sick of them. And then, in the summer of 1914, a fancy to see the Old Country. He had worked his passage homeward in a short-handed tramp and arrived at Tilbury on the day the Kaiser's government sent its ultimatum to Russia. Four days later he was a soldier in the British Army, and a year or so later had a knee-cap damaged and a shoulder put out of action. They had patched him up carefully, made quite a decent job of him, and he walked and moved his left arm with comfort; but, adjudged unfit for the fighting line, he had done with the trenches for good. Permanent base now, with a cushy job at the office of the D.D. of Works. Filing and copying documents relating to hut construction; he had been fool enough to let out that he had had some small training as a clerk.

"In a way," he said, chewing at a long blade of grass, "it's a good thing I've got my stiff knee. If I could put the miles under me as I used to, I believe—I believe I'd go. It would come over me and I'd go. Not that I want to desert, but it might be too strong for me; I've always been my own master and I've always wanted to know what was on the other side of the hill. Straight on"—he pointed southward—"straight on, anywhere. The road—if you've once tramped it" ... He broke off and stared with his eyes on the distance and beyond it.

After a minute or two of silence he asked William suddenly what had made him join the Army; and William gave him confidence for confidence, attracted he knew not why. The man's craving for loneliness and bodily exertion was something he could not understand; but they were on common ground in their mutual rebellion against the weariness of daily life. They talked with long silences in between their speech, telling out their hearts to each other; or rather finding in each other's presence an excuse for speaking their hearts. Later it seemed odd to William that though they spoke freely of their lives and their griefs it had never struck either of them to ask of the other his name.

"So you joined up because of your wife," said the man who lay on his elbow.

"Yes," William answered him, "I thought——" He did not finish the sentence; it wearied him now to remember what he had thought.

"Sometimes," the other broke the silence, "I ask myself why I joined up. Don't see how it could have been patriotism; England hadn't been anything to me for years. My sister died soon after I left it and I hadn't any one else. So far as I can make out it never was much to me; I was always unhappy in England, hated school and office and towns—I lived in a town. Never knew what life could be till I got away from it. Say the Germans had won and dominated the earth! They wouldn't have dominated my earth. I could always have made myself a camp-fire where they wouldn't have wanted to follow me. If they'd sacked London and swallowed up New York I could have lain out under the stars at night and laughed at 'em. So what made me? ... Some say man's a fighting animal."

He pulled a fresh grass-blade to chew and rolled over on his chest till his chin rested on his hands.

"I knew I should hate soldiering—I made no mistake about that. The regularity—shipboard's too regular for me. I've tried it more than once for the sake of getting somewhere, and before the voyage was half over I'd always had more than enough. I knew I should hate it, but I joined up straight and away.... I've lost everything that made life good to me. Other chaps—blind chaps and crippled—might think I'd got off easily. So I have, I daresay; but then it isn't every one whose life was in moving on. Often when I was alone I've shouted and laughed just to feel how my legs moved under me.... It's the devil—this compound—but even if I were out of it, I'm a lame thing. When the war ends I'm a lame thing. Not what most people would call crippled, of course; I can walk a few miles and feed myself, and to look at me you wouldn't know there was anything at all the matter. If I were a townsman it wouldn't make very much difference; if I'd stayed a clerk I could go on being a clerk. But I can't be ... what I was. I've lost everything that made life good to me. What for?

"I can't remember exactly the feeling I had about it when I enlisted—what made me do it. So many things have happened since then. But I know I didn't think about it long; so far as I remember I didn't hesitate, not for a minute. I went straight off the morning after war was declared. Midnight, fourth, we were at war, and midday, fifth, I was a soldier. Must have been some sort of instinct.... Sometimes I tell myself what a blazing fool I am.

"That's sometimes. Other times— —"

He was silent for so long that William concluded the flow of his confidence had ceased.

"When you live in a crowd," he said at last, "you can always make excuses for yourself. Most likely you don't need to. If you're a fool or a coward you herd with a lot of other fools and cowards, and you all back each other up. So you never come face to face with yourself."

The idea was new to William, and a year or two ago he would have repelled it because it was new; now he turned his eyes from the horizon, curiously, to the lean brown face at his elbow.

"No?" he said interrogatively.

"If," said the other, "if I had gone back ... it wouldn't have been the same. It couldn't have been.... If you live that way there's two things you can't do without: a good strong body to stand rain and wind and work, and a mind you're not afraid to be alone with. When you're miles from any one, in the woods at night, you want to be good company for yourself. If I'd turned my back on it all, I mightn't have been very good company. I've done plenty of things to set the parsons praying over me if I told 'em; I've been a fool times out of mind and ashamed of it afterwards; but— —"

He slid into a silence that lasted until William took up the word; not in answer or argument but irrelevantly, so that he, too, might talk out his heart.

"Do you know what I think I am sometimes? a rat in a trap—or a squirrel spinning round in a cage. Very busy doing nothing.... I'll tell you one of the things I've been doing lately—every word of it truth. I've been typing a long correspondence about a civilian—a worker in one of the religious organizations who came into the town, ten miles by train, to get stores he wanted for his hut. The rule is, civilians mustn't travel by train without a movement order from the A.P.M.; there isn't an A.P.M. in the place he comes from, so he went to the military and got an *ordre de service*.

He came all right, but it's irregular—an *ordre de service* should only be given to a soldier. One of the M.P.'s on duty at the station reported it—and there's been strafing and strafing and strafing. Reams written about it—I've written 'em. Not only about the *ordre de service* but about who the correspondence is to go through—the A.P.M.'s office or the Base Commandant or some one else. After three or four weeks it was referred to G.H.Q. and some one there wrote to the secretary of the organization asking for an explanation—and naturally he answered the letter. Well, that was irregular too; he oughtn't to have answered because the matter should have been dealt with locally—'gone through the proper channels.' So more correspondence and strafing.... Sheets of paper—reams of it—and they say it's scarce! And in the end, nothing—just nothing. When the wretched people wrote and asked exactly what they were to do—how they were to get a movement order from an A.P.M. when there wasn't an A.P.M. to give it, we wrote back and said, 'This correspondence must now cease.' I ticked it out on my typewriter."

"I believe you," the other nodded, "I've seen something of that sort myself.... And the papers say, 'Your country wants you'!"

"And it goes on," said William, "day after day. I'm always busy—about nothing. 'Attention is directed to G.R.O. 9999. The Return called for in the form shown as the third appendix——'"

"Good Lord," cried the other, "stop it. That's just what maddens me—I don't want to think of it."

William laughed sullenly with his chin resting on his hand.

"I've not much else to think of," he said.

He watched the lean man down the hill till a winding of the road hid him; and then he too rose, in his turn, and went back to the town—to the rat-trap wherein he made war!

CHAPTER XVIII

The war was well past its third anniversary when William again met Edith Haynes. The silence once broken between them they had corresponded with a fair regularity, and, leave being due to him, he wrote to ask if he should be likely to meet her in London; receiving in answer a hearty invitation to pass as much of his leave as he could spare—the whole of it if he would—with her mother and herself in Somerset. The reply was an eager acceptance; hitherto his leave, if a respite from the office, had been dreary enough in comparison with the home-comings of other men—it was a suspicion of the loneliness in which it was usually passed that had prompted Edith's invitation. She met him at the station and drove him home, and they picked up their odd friendship at the point where they had left it off.

The only other member of the family with whom he made acquaintance was a delicate, pale mother, given, since her firstborn was killed at Thiepval, to long silences and lonely brooding; a younger son had been a prisoner since the surrender at Kut, and Edith ran her mother as well as the house and the estate. She looked older, and by more than the passing of three years; the iron of war had entered into her soul, for the brother killed in France had been her darling as well as her mother's; but in other ways she was just what William remembered her, a kindly and capable good comrade. The delicate, pale mother kept much to her room, and the pair, in consequence, were left often to each other's company—sometimes tramping the home farm with Edith bent on bailiff's duties, sometimes sitting by the evening fire. For the first day or two he was not communicative—engrossed, perhaps, in mere pleasure in his new surroundings; but even through the stiffness and restraint of his letters she had guessed at something of the change that had come over him, and when he showed signs of emerging from his shell she took pains, on her side, to draw him out and discover his attitude of mind. By degrees, from his silences as much as from his speech, she learned of the weariness that had settled like a mist on his soul, the aimlessness with which he plodded the pathway of his disciplined life. She knew him for a man disillusioned, in whom the imaginings of his pre-soldier days had died as completely as his faith in his pre-war creed. Had the lot fallen to him he would not have shrunk from his turn in the trenches, and at the bottom of his heart, for Griselda's sake, there was always a smoulder of hatred;

but he had seen much of the war machine, had realized keenly his own unimportance therein, and he blushed when he remembered that he had once imagined that his one small arm and his private vengeance might be factors, and important factors, in the downfall of the German Empire. And the first mad impulse of agony, the impulse which would have sent him into battle single-handed, had passed as it was bound to pass.

If she suspected him at first of a drift towards his former "pacifism" she soon discovered her mistake; the one rock on which he stood fast was that conviction of error which had come to him in the Forest of Arden. He hated the war as it affected himself, was weary of the war in general; all he longed for was its ending, which meant his release from imprisonment; but neither hatred nor weariness had blinded his eyes to the folly of that other blindness which had denied that war could be. His contempt for his past dreams of a field-marshal's baton was as nothing to his contempt for those further past dreams wherein fact was dispelled by a theory; and he had, in his own words, "no use for" a pacifist party which had never, as he had, made confession of its fundamental error. He was still in his heart a soldier, even though a soldier disillusioned; his weariness of the military machine, his personal grievance against it, were not to be compared to the fiery conversion that had followed on the outbreak of war. The one concerned matters of detail only; the other his fundamental faith.... So much Edith Haynes understood from their intimate fragmentary talks.

One change in himself he had not noticed till Edith, half jestingly, spoke of it: an affection that was almost a tenderness for the actual soil of England. More than once when he walked with her he contrasted the road or the landscape with those grown familiar in France; and the contrast was always in favour of the Somerset hills or the winding Somerset highway. Without ties as he was, without household, without family, she saw that he shrank from the idea of again leaving "home."

"What shall you do when the war is over?" she asked him one evening as his leave neared its end, curious to know how he had planned to spend his arrested life. So far he had spoken of no future beyond the end of the war itself; and when she put to him the question direct he only shook his head vaguely.

"I don't know. It may seem odd to you, but I haven't thought much about it. In fact"—he smiled apologetically—"I don't believe I've really thought at all."

"No, I don't think it odd," she told him. "There are a good many like you—I'm inclined to think that you're only one of the majority. People whose business it is to reorganize industry—I suppose they're thinking ahead. One prays they are. But as for the rest of us ... it's difficult to think ahead because of the way it has broken up our lives and our plans. We've got used to its breaking them up."

"That's it," he nodded back. "We've been made to do things for so long. Taken and made to do them.... Some have been taken and killed and some have been taken and crushed—and some have only been made prisoners, like me. But we've all of us been taken—and bent and twisted into things we never meant to be.... So we don't plan—what's the use? ... I might of course—I'm not like the men in the trenches who may be killed any minute. I'm safe enough where I am—safer than in London; but all the same I don't.... I just wait to see what happens."

For a week before William left England there had been expectation of coming developments at the front, and the papers had spoken of "considerable aerial activity," on the enemy's side as on ours. The developments commenced in earnest on the day of his return from leave; but his first personal experience of the increase in aerial activity was not for a few days later, when, as he was passing through the square in the centre of the town, a gun thudded out—and then another. He stopped and made one of a little knot of khaki that was staring up into the blue, and whereof one of the component parts was a corporal who worked in his office. He himself could see nothing but a drift or two of smoke, but he gathered from the sharper-sighted corporal that there were two Fritz planes overhead, and he stood cricking his neck and blinking upwards in the strong sunlight while passers-by made groups on the pavement and shopkeepers issued from their doors. He had seen the same thing happen before and quite harmlessly; no one around him seemed alarmed or disturbed, and in a few minutes the guns ceased firing as the aeroplanes passed out of range.

"Photographing," said the corporal, as they walked away to the office. "He's been over quite a lot the last week or two, and some time or other I suppose we shall have him in earnest. It's a wonder to me he's left us alone so long; it 'ud be worth his while coming even if he didn't do more than drop a bomb or two on the A.H.T.D., and start a few hundred horses."

"Yes," agreed William, "I suppose it would." He was not in the least alarmed as he settled down to his files; since he joined the Army he had never been exposed to danger, and security had become with him a habit.

That night there was a heavy post, and the office was kept working late; it was close on eleven when William was called upstairs to take down some letters from dictation. The officer who had sent for him was clearing his throat for the first sentence when the door opened for the announcement, "Local aircraft alarm, sir."

"Oh, all right," said the officer resignedly. "Go downstairs, Tully, and come up again when the lights go on. Probably only a false alarm—we had two the other night. Just the sort of thing that would happen when we're behindhand."

He went out grumbling, and William followed him, feeling his way by the banisters, for the electric light was turned off while he was still on the upper landing; other men from all over the warren of a building were descending likewise, and they bumped and jostled each other in the sudden darkness on the stairs. There were jests as they bumped and much creaking of boots—through which, while William was still a flight from the ground floor, came the first rapid thudding of "Archie." On it, a moment later, an unmistakable bomb and the pattering outburst of machine-guns.... William listened curiously; it was his first experience of an air raid, and though the pace of his heart quickened, as yet there was no real fear in him; but a man pressed against him by the descending stream gasped audibly and clawed round William's arm with his fingers. The action was fear made manifest in darkness, and William, instinctively knowing it infectious, repelled it and strove to free his wrist; but the shaking fingers, eloquent of terror, only clung more tightly to their hold.

"What is it?" William snapped. "What's the matter?"

"It's me—Wright," a voice whispered back in jerks. "I can't help it—the Lord knows I try, but I can't. If it was shells I could stand 'em, but——"

A near-by gun beat down his voice but did not stop it—"at Dunkirk. I was buried two hours: two mortal hours before they got me out—and when I was in hospital he came over and bombed us again. He got one right on to us, and I was blown out of bed, and the men at the other end of the ward were in pieces. In pieces, I tell you—beastly bits of flesh——"

William tried to stand it—realizing that the man must cling and gibber to some one as a child clings and wails to its nurse. They had turned into a room on the ground floor—there were no cellars, but it was esteemed the safest place in the building by reason of the comparative absence of glass—and the pair of them stood backs against the wall. When Wright stopped talking—which was not often—William could hear his breath as it came whining through his teeth; and he remembered that the man wore the ribbon of the D.C.M.—a man who had once had nerve and to all appearance was sound, but who had not sufficient hold on himself to keep his terror from his tongue. He spoke of it unceasingly; whenever the sounds without died down William could hear him whispering—now of the night when he was bombed in hospital and now of the building they were in. It was no good as a shelter—would crumble like a house of cards. Nothing was any good but a cellar or trenches—there should have been trenches. And they were so damnably close to the station, and the station was just what those devils were trying to hit. There came a moment when William could bear it no more, and wrenched himself free of the clawing fingers on his sleeve; he dared not feel them longer, lest his heart also melted within him.

His nervousness took the form of a difficulty in keeping still, and he fidgeted about the darkened room; but the room was fairly full, and he could not move far—after a step or two this way and a step or two that, he was brought up by a solid group that stretched from the wall to a table. He came to a standstill on the edge of the group and tried to listen to their talk; forced himself to listen to it—and all the time straining his ears through the murmur for the droning of the Gotha engines. He fought with himself and fought more manfully than he knew; striving to thrust out of his mind Wright's phrase about the "beastly bits of flesh," and to fasten his hearing, to the exclusion of all else, on the voice of a man, his neighbour in the darkness, who had lately seen a German aeroplane brought down, and, having apparently some mechanical knowledge, was describing its points and its engines. They, the engines, were first-rate, he said, waxing technical; but even if he had not been told it, he should have guessed from the fittings of the plane that Jerry was getting a bit scarce in his stock of rubber and leather. What he was using— — Here the windows rattled loudly and drowned him. "That's pretty close," some one commented, and William moved a restless step away. Once it had seemed to him an easy thing to follow Griselda and die; now all the moral strength he possessed went into the effort not to shrink, to be master of his body, to behave decently and endure. That was all that seemed to matter—to be steady and behave decently—so that, for all his fear of instant death, he never turned his thoughts to God.... He had not known how beautiful silence could be till it came almost suddenly, like a flood of clear, cool water; when some one, muttering that it seemed to be over, opened the door and went out into the courtyard, he followed and stood there feeling the silence as something clean, exquisite and grateful. His hands were wet and hot, and he stretched them out to the air; if he had not prayed when he was under the spell of fear, his heart, at his release from it, was filled with something like praise.

"Listen," said a voice in his ear. It was Wright, his face uplifted in the moonlight and disfigured by ugly twitchings. "Listen," he said, "they're coming back." ... William shrank from him irritably, but the man had not spoken particularly to him, and, having spoken, turned swiftly and went back into the house. He had been the first to catch the double-noted drone which as they stood and listened grew nearer.

x

x

"That's him, sure enough," another voice agreed. "Coming up in relays. He'll be out to make a night of it — I thought we'd got rid of him too quickly."

A searchlight wheeled and the anti-aircraft spoke on the word; some one cried, "Got 'im," and pointed, and for an instant William had sight of a wicked thing caught in the ray and rushing upwards. Battery and machine-gun gave tongue at the sight, but in a flash the climbing devil had vanished and the searchlight wheeled after it fruitlessly. As they stood and watched it wheeling, a voice called, "Come in, men," and they went back perforce within their walls.

The first attack had lasted not much over half an hour; this time the ordeal by darkness and waiting was longer. William held himself tightly, ashamed of the weakness with which Wright had infected him and keeping it doggedly at bay; he talked when he could think of anything to talk about — odd irrelevant fragments of whatever came into his head, anything to keep himself from listening. At one time he made a conscious and determined effort to turn his talk and his mind with it to something unconnected with air-raids; but always his speech, like that of his companions, came back to the thought of the moment.

"Do you remember," he asked a man beside him, "what a fuss there was about the first Channel flight? I forget the fellow's name — a Frenchman?"

Some one supplied the name, "Bleriot," out of the darkness.

"Yes, Bleriot — that's it.... Queer when you think of it. Nobody had any idea then what it would mean — getting into cellars and hiding in the dark. If they had" — he forced an attempt at a laugh — "they wouldn't have been so pleased."

"No," his neighbour agreed with him jocularly; "they wouldn't have been so pleased. We thought we was all going to flap about like birds — and instead the most of us go scuttling into holes like beetles what the cook's trying to stamp on. That's flying — for them as don't fly."

"Yes," said William, "that's flying." The beetle simile caught his fancy oddly, and he found himself contrasting it with his old idea of a soldier. After all, the beetle-warrior was a new development — it was impossible to think of Napoleonic heroes as beetles. Yet if they were alive they would have to scuttle too — even Murat the magnificent, and Ney, the Red Lion ...

"When the next war comes," his jocular neighbour was continuing, "every man that ain't in the R.F.C. 'ull be crawling at the bottom of a coal-mine. And I don't mind mentioning in confidence that if I saw a coal-mine 'andy I wouldn't mind crawling down it now."

"No," said William, for the sake of speaking, "I don't suppose you would." He was trying to think of something further to say when he felt the man on his other side start perceptibly and stiffen in attention. Something caught at his throat and he could only whisper, "What is it?"

"He's stopping his engine," said the other quietly; and before William had time to ask what he meant the next bomb fell in the courtyard.

There was only one man wholly uninjured—the terror-haunted Wright, who ran out, splashed with other men's blood, took screaming to his heels and collapsed a mile along the road. There he lay till long after the bell of St. Nicholas had rung an "All Clear" to the town—until long after the ambulances telephoned for from the hospitals outside had loaded up in the streets across which cordons had been drawn by military police and French firemen. Men and fragments of men were taken from the ruins, some speedily, some after much search; and among them Private Tully, past terror, but breathing, still alive but only alive.

He spoke but a few times after the explosion had broken him, and the men who lifted him on a stretcher to the ambulance and out of it could see that he suffered not at all; the shifting and handling that was torture to others left his maimed and mauled body unaffected. The injury to the spine that was killing him had bereft him of the power of pain as well as of the power of movement, and in the hospital, where a few minutes' drive from the ruins landed him, he lay quietly alive for a day or two, for the most part dumb and unconscious, but with intervals of sense and lucid speech. Once, in such an interval, he whispered to the nurse that his wife, too, was buried in France; whereby she saw that he knew he was about to die.

Later he asked that some one would write to Edith Haynes, and tried to explain who she was. "No relation—just a lady I know.... I should like her to hear."

The last person he spoke to was a chaplain, a young man making his round of the ward, who, seeing intelligence in the pale blue eyes, bent over the bed to ask if there was anything he wanted. The chaplain had been warned by a sister that here was a hopeless case, and he spoke very gently and bent very low for the answer.

It drifted out faintly in a slow and expressionless whisper.

"No, thank you," said William. "I don't seem to have been much good ... but there comes a time ... when nothing matters."

"Not even," asked the chaplain, feeling his way, "the sense that you have done your duty?"

"Most people do that," said William. "The question is ... if you've been much use when you've done it."

The chaplain, puzzled, said something of infinite mercy and the standard of God not being as the standard of man.

"If you've done your best..." he suggested.

"Most people do that," said William again ... and slid back once more into silence.

He was buried without mourners, save those detailed for the duty; who, none the less, stiffened in salute of his coffin and called him farewell on the bugle. His death, duly entered in the hospital books, was reported to the Casualty Department; and the Graves Registration clerks took note of his burial and filed it for possible inquiries.

www.ingramcontent.com/pod-product-compliance
Lightning Source LLC
LaVergne TN
LVHW041809170325
806140LV00035B/637